# THE LEGACY SERIES

Series Titles

*The Spirit in My Shoes*
John Michael Cummings

*Maximum Speed*
Kevin Clouther

*Reach Her in This Light*
Jane Curtis

*The Effects of Urban Renewal on Mid-Century America and Other Crime Stories*
Jeff Esterholm

*What Makes You Think You're Supposed to Feel Better*
Jody Hobbs Hesler

*Fugitive Daydreams*
Leah McCormack

*Hoist House: A Novella & Stories*
Jenny Robertson

*Finding the Bones: Stories & A Novella*
Nikki Kallio

*Self-Defense*
Corey Mertes

*Where Are Your People From?*
James B. De Monte

*Sometimes Creek*
Steve Fox

*The Plagues*
Joe Baumann

Praise for
*The Spirit in My Shoes*

"John Michael Cummings's debut collection, *The Spirit in My Shoes*, showcases twenty-three sharply drawn stories that seamlessly dip and dive into various times, spaces, and unexpected glimpses of colorful lives, knitting together a collective human experience that's alternatingly funny, touching, and at times surprising, but wholly satisfying in its weight and depth."

—Kali White
author of *The Monsters We Make*

"A remarkable collection of stories thrumming with subtle probing humor and quiet insight, these visceral narratives of a clear honest voice become a knife cutting through to the heart with masterful skill and insight, making lived experience into theater, moments timeless, ephemeral yet indelible, unveiling the universe in the mind, the cosmos in the home, and the world of the neighborhood."

—Aimee Parkison
author of *Girl Zoo*

"The stories in John Michael Cummings's *The Spirit in My Shoes* portray our basest human instincts set against the deepest yearnings of our hearts. These characters, all misfits in one way or another, are both vulnerable and strong, fearful and brave. In "Genetic Drift," a grotesque boy dares the odds of his survival. In "Fourteen Seconds," the death of John Kennedy Jr. becomes the metaphor for a dying relationship. In "Crows and Sparrows," the narrator says, 'We're all dying, Linda, dying in spirit.' Yet in the flawed, indomitable spirits of these characters, we see ourselves. An unforgettable collection."

—Gerry Wilson
author of *Crosscurrents and Other Stories*

"Is it possible for the removal of earwax to be sexy? Absolutely, if the tale is written by John Michael Cummings. *The Spirit in My Shoes* is not only a fine collection of short stories but a deeply human one, whether Cummings is delving into the boisterous psyche of a bicycle-racing boy or how the death of John F. Kennedy, Jr. embroils a couple in the oddest of ways. The title story, a flash fiction piece, somehow manages to be both lyrical and hilarious, while in the final story, "Every Living Thing," Cummings showcases his dramatic brio in the aftermath of a windstorm (those poor downed trees, so lovingly depicted). A wonderfully thoughtful work by an obvious master of the short form."

—Sung J. Woo
author of *Skin Deep* and *Everything Asian*

"In his debut story collection—*The Spirit in My Shoes*—John Michael Cummings ignites every page with insight and imagination. He delivers the world in all its complexity, illuminating the travails of the forlorn, the lost, the beloved, the desperate, the coupled (happily and not so), the childish, the cynical, the joyful, the confused. In the wide range of Cummings's concerns, readers will find not only much to contemplate but also much to celebrate."

—Ron Tanner
author of *Far West* and *Missile Paradise*

"In three decades of vibrant and luminous stories set against the backdrop of historic Harpers Ferry, West Virginia, novelist John Michael Cummings's debut collection, *The Spirit in My Shoes*, trains his distinctive eye for *moeurs domestique* on the community he knows best—and does so with a fierce optimism that captures the abiding promise of the human spirit. These are nuanced stories of magnitude and deep emotional truth. Every one of these twenty-three literary treasures is inventive, honest to the bone, and well worth the wait. A must read for the serious connoisseur of contemporary short fiction."

—Jacob M. Appel
author of *Einstein's Beach House*

"John Michael Cummings writes stories that bristle with secret heartbreak. In *The Spirit in My Shoes*, tales of isolation, longing, and occasional huge triumphs come to life on the page. Cummings's lively, complex, poignant, and often surprisingly funny stories have settings that range wide across the eastern U.S., but they all seem to bubble up from a deep wellspring of hard-won experience. I dare readers to put one down unfinished, and I dare writer/readers not to feel inspired to rush to the computer to write a few new stories themselves."

—Jean Anderson
author of *Human Being Songs: Northern Stories*

"Those who read the best contemporary lit mags, where John Michael Cummings has been publishing his inimitable fiction for decades, will want to get their hands on his new collection straightaway. I'm glad I did. For those who do not yet know his work, the stories in this book will serve well as an introduction."

—Christopher Chambers
author of *Kind of Blue* and *Delta 88*

"Deploying his spare but elegant prose in *The Spirit in My Shoes*, John Michael Cummings reaches for the heavens in a couple dozen tales featuring not-quite suburbanites in some "historic" American villages now drained of their authenticity by touristy restoration. Somehow, using little more than a few declarative sentences, Cummings can make hidden sensual longing, racial tension, and class resentment drive tense narratives of flawed but attractive characters facing significant moments in their expressly quotidian lives. Gorgeous writing; memorable stories; fine art."

—Charles Lamar Phillips
author of *Estranged* and *Dead South*

"An engrossing collection of stories that speaks to life's larger and softer questions."

—Dina S. Rabadi
author of *Peter's Moonlight Photography and Other Stories*

"If Flannery O'Connor and John Updike hadn't been encumbered by religion, they could have produced stories like these. With versatility that takes the reader from a headstone maker to an artist who plays with the meaning of black-and-white, Cummings defies us to read any story just once."

—Patty Friedmann
author of *Too Jewish* and *Secondhand Smoke*

"John Michael Cummings's *The Spirit in My Shoes* reminds us about the power of literature to not only activate our senses, but challenge us to reclaim our humanity in a darkling age. Cummings' stories takes readers on a journey through our vexed and vexing contemporary age, where, if we look hard enough, we might yet find our way through the morass."

—Kenneth Womack
author of *I Am Lemonade Lucy!*

"John Michael Cummings is full of surprises in the elements he connects, in what people say and do, and in his undermining of the seemingly likely. Several of the stories dramatize variations of relationships on the brink of failure, misadventures that, in a more typical short story, would drive a couple apart. But Cummings has the ability to reverse expectations convincingly, without tricks or sentimentality."

—Walter Cummins
author of *Telling Stories: Old & New* and *The End of the Circle*

"In this remarkable collection of twenty-three stories, some flash, some more expansive, John Michael Cummings makes action symbol, and location destiny. A grocery store, a church: no matter how mundane, there is no place to hide. With precise language and sharply-drawn characters, *The Spirit in My Shoes* pleases as much as it unsettles, and that's quite an achievement."

—Tim Tomlinson
author of *This Is Not Happening to You*

"These cozy little domestic disturbances that John Michael Cummings has, like killer crabs and three-legged crows, kicking about the heels of his Converse Chuck Taylors are sure to keep you off balance and entertained for days on end; and for that matter, you'll be relieved that his little domestic desserts full of surprise, suspense, life, death, and a little bit of Bar Harbor homemade whipped cream for blueberry pie are so very damn good."

—Jéanpaul Ferro
author of *The Knife of Never Letting Go* and *Torchlight Parade*

"These striking, incisive stories explore with insight relationships (and loneliness) in 21st-century America: relationships between couples, between parents and children, between the living and the dead. You will come away from reading John Michael Cummings's book enlightened and deeply moved."

—Fred Waage
author of *This Mortal Earth: A Year of Beginnings and Ceasings*

"*The Spirit in My Shoes*, John Michael Cummings's excellent new story collection, begins with a couple exploring the meaning of trust, and ends with another couple surveying the aftermath of a freak summer wind storm. In between, Cummings treats us to tales of old love, new love, lost love, love in all its complexity. His keen ear for dialogue takes us up and down the East Coast, often to the West Virginia panhandle. I learned from, and enjoyed, these twenty-three stories. I'd bet you will too."

—Ken Waldman
author of *Now Entering Alaska Time*

"John Michael Cummings's collection, like all fine craftwork, best reveals itself through close inspection. The stories pose hard questions that tease out our own doubts, failings, and those sweet memories we long to return to, but seem to neglect. *The Spirit in My Shoes* invites the reader—often via subtle emotional provocation—to compare themselves to characters struggling to escape self-imposed torments."

—Mitchell Toews
author of *Pinching Zwieback*

"Those readers already familiar with aspects of this author's life will recognize John Michael Cummings's masterful adaptations of autobiographical details melded into these compelling stories. Writing in the literary realist tradition of Steinbeck and Updike, Cummings examines articulately and poignantly through his characters and their circumstances the universal longing within the human heart for connectedness, understanding, and, yes, love."

—Mark Scheel
author of *And Eve Said Yes: Seven Stories and a Novella*

"John Michael Cummings's domestic, urban, and road-based settings envelop the reader in a landscape of eccentric psyches on the brink of change. In his stories, talk and textured language drive characters to visceral conclusions, forcing them to choose whether they have landed in complete despair or a future with the possibility of hope. Each story is an invitation to discovery, and a ride worth taking."

—Joshua Wetjen
author of "Currents" and "Synesthesia"

# The Spirit in My Shoes

Stories

### John Michael Cummings

Cornerstone Press
*Stevens Point, Wisconsin*

Cornerstone Press, Stevens Point, Wisconsin 54481
Copyright © 2023 John Michael Cummings
www.uwsp.edu/cornerstone

Printed in the United States of America by
Point Print and Design Studio, Stevens Point, Wisconsin

Library of Congress Control Number: 2023940037
ISBN: 978-1-960329-10-3



Cornerstone Press titles are produced in courses and internships offered by the Department of English at the University of Wisconsin–Stevens Point.

DIRECTOR & PUBLISHER   EXECUTIVE EDITOR
Dr. Ross K. Tangedal      Jeff Snowbarger

SENIOR EDITORS
Lexie Neeley, Monica Swinick, Kala Buttke

PRESS STAFF
Carolyn Czerwinski, Grace Dahl, Zoie Dinehart, Kirsten Faulkner, Brett Hill, Kenzie Kierstyn, Natalie Reiter, Arianna Soto, Anthony Thiel, Chloe Verhelst

*To the late poet and English professor Mark Craver,*<br>*who encouraged me to write.*

Also by John Michael Cummings:

*The Night I Freed John Brown*
*Ugly To Start With*
*Don't Forget Me, Bro*

# Stories

# Like Apes

Lowering her head onto his lap, Lisa realized she'd never fully trusted him. She felt uneasy—afraid. His request to clean her ears, this manner of penetration, was strange, raw, and darkly sexual of him. At the same time, it was utterly innocent and candidly paternal. After all, he just cleaned the Lab's deep grimy ears. During the procedure of dirtying the tip of a cotton swab, using the other end, then discarding, he fancied himself the responsible husband with everyone's ears, the family dog now finished and his wife next.

Having surrendered her head to his lap, would he now behead her? Steeling herself, she cocked her ear to the realm of exposure. How would a Q-tip feel handled by him?

"Ready?" he asked.

As soon as it entered—itchy, noisy, and immediately lethal—she seized his legs, bracing for pain.

"Now, hold still, honey," he reminded her patiently, his wife situated vulnerably across his thighs. Meanwhile, panting, smiling Sammy the Labrador had taken his place on the sofa, his tongue falling from his mouth.

"Don't hurt me," she plainly warned, shutting her eyes.

He paused.

"You trust me, don't you?"

She refused him an answer. With her eyes shut, the darkness spotlighted the feeling of the cotton swab as it softly bulldozed the irregular grooves of her ear, working through the wiggling ruts of cartilage. Her legs, arms, and scalp—all tingled. When the Q-tip plunged into the ear canal, as if ramrodding inside her head, she shivered. He stopped.

"Honey."

"I'm holding still," she grimaced. "Let's just get this over with."

Meanwhile, Sammy was watching her with a tilted, inquisitive face, his tongue pleasantly inside.

"You're pretty clean," her husband soon announced, sounding impressed. He removed the swab entirely from the elastic funnel of her ear. "No wax at all."

"I told you," she bragged, pinching his leg.

He leaned close again.

"Nope. Wait. Here. Just found a lot of gunk."

She sighed while silly Sammy unfurled his tongue again. When she told her dog to stop breathing on her, he flapped his muscly tail on an unruffled section of the Sunday paper on the sofa beside her. She opened her eyes to see a headline staring at her. She droned, "U.S. Divorce Rate Rockets – 3 of 5 Marriages Fail.'"

"Really?" he asks. "Three?"

His voice, though spoken in a normal tone, boomed into her ear, setting off tremors through her head.

"That's what it says…'more than a million divorces last year alone.'"

"Babylon."

"No, the United States."

"But not us."

"Yes, us. If not careful."

He squirmed. Raised Catholic, they had always viewed themselves to be too honorable for divorce, too decent and faithful.

"Twice as much as Canada," she added.

"No surprise there—wait, did you say a million?"

"Yup, mister, and keep cleaning."

When he carelessly sent what felt like a toothbrush into her ear canal, she pushed him away and sat up.

"Jack, not so far in. I just told you."

The dog, having just lowered his head onto his front paws, now reared his boxy black muzzle, not sure which of them to frown at.

"I'm not that far in," he defended.

"I wish you'd be that far in somewhere else."

"Behave. Wax builds up in here—you'll have serious ear problems if I don't get it out," he said, trying to sound like an authority with a prognosis. Then, he swatted her tush. "Don't jerk away from me like that!"

Slowly, she surrendered her ear to him again, miffed and all the leerier. Turning horizontally, she observed bookshelves, doors, and tables all pivoted synchronously to the right and perched on a perpendicular axis. The standing sofa, suspended vases, and open areas of walls arranged like monstrous clamps holding together the components of their house—all spun her mind into wondrous oblivion.

Don't jerk, flinch, or wiggle, she was ordered again. So she obeyed. While the Q-tip explored her head like an automated probe, she relaxed and read the newspaper, well, like a newspaper.

"'…result of a lack of emotional support and general diverging interests…'"

"General, diverging interests, huh? Like if you start ridin' a Harley?"

"Honey, listen to this—" Bumping him away yet again, she raised her head to read more easily. "—the honesty and trust of the mate—'"

"Mate? It says that? Like apes?"

"Stop interrupting—'are essentials missing from a marriage...'" She dropped her head flat on his knees, asking the unanswerable, "How can people just become that way?"

"Because they don't clean each other's ears?"

She elbowed him.

"Stop it. Seriously, how can two people in love become so bitter and fierce with each other?"

Briefly, they both fell silent, the great question of humanity asked.

Sammy, up on two paws with his nose glistening and wriggling, had stretched far enough to see where the funny clear-blue stick was poking.

The scratchy microphonic crackle of the cotton tip—free to impact the vulnerable center of the pinna—encircled the ear canal with the rotational speed of a can caught on the edge of a whirlpool, drawn into the dark, dropping center.

It tickled the fuzz in her inner ear and excited the sensitive surface of the pinkest, innermost skin. Once, she prepared for pain while he seemed inches inside her, wedging and pushing, as if using a digging iron. The sensation of stimulated nerves nearly rendered her spasmodic.

"More men than women commit adultery," she continued.

"No way."

"Says so here."

She read aloud until he interrupted, telling her to change sides, one ear finished. When she did, her uncleaned ear arose as the dirty half of her she wanted him to handle more firmly this time. All the while, her cleaned ear greeted the volume, pitch, and tone of his voice.

"Trust is a big part," she murmured, relaxing, ready for him now.

Swab after swab looped and lapped and backtracked the supple channels and depressions of her ear. The experience felt as electrically orgasmic as when his fingertips kneaded the tight knots of muscles of her neck.

"Mmm," she groaned.

She kept her eyes closed while the tip of the swab swayed her head like currents of water. Once, when she moaned, Sammy yelped, confused. She yearned for Jack to enter her canal opening, to press upon what felt like an erotic pressure point.

Finally, she let him quit, and when he stood, she roused herself and announced, "Okay, now your turn," and pulled him back onto the sofa. "Trust me."

# Genetic Drift

Whoever lives on this narrow seaside street surely wonders why the little blond boy furiously bicycling the sidewalks yells hellishly at whomever he targets between his kiddie-green handlebars. His strident and indeterminate shouts penetrate the flanking rows of varnished Colonial apartments, and when he hollers while passing the lowest row of windows on the far side of his street, his wild shouts catch a cavity of air and resound like sirens in the night.

On the corner closest to his house stands a plain, folkish dwelling rented to surfers every summer. When the little boy, about five or so, speeds past its low windows in the early evening, the surfers yell from inside, "Way to go, Alex!" In the morning, they bark, "Shut the hell up, boy!"

But he ignores anyone he has seen up close for more than a few moments. He wants to be anywhere but here.

Whenever tourists meander up his street, he darts toward them, demanding, "Wh-where is you going?"

As seen from the double sashes in the dusty yellow Greek Revival house commanding his intersection, little Alex dares the traffic beyond the stop sign. His small, fluorescent green bike charges into the crossroads of danger, where he circles and coasts. His stubby, pink legs stretch to his sides, his dinky feet on the pedals. When he finally drifts back onto his quiet side street, he immediately prepares for another perilous dash through traffic.

He tacks, sprints, and skids serpentine along the sidewalks for hours. Shirtless, his jointless little arms smack the sticky plants growing where the buildings crowd the walks. If he spots a surfer leaving the house, he dashes into the large driveway shared by three houses and stomps on the coaster brakes, yelling, "Wh-where is you going?"

"Out."

"But why?"

"Because…"

A grape-colored Jeep roars to life beside his little engineless bike, belching black exhaust fumes across his pink legs, exciting him. He sits in the fumes, panting, listening to the gunning engine, to the bursting crackle of the radio. The tanned surfer drags a shirt from his back, ready to hit the waves.

"I race you, y-you son of a bitc-hh," little Alex stutters in a combusting racket. But if even someone hears him, he so excites himself that his incoherent words exit his mouth like a handful of flung coins. "I race you, bit-cch."

The popping Jeep backs out of the driveway, sucking gravel under its tires, and Alex follows, his tiny front tire wobbling as he pedals furiously to catch the big purple machine. Yelling, he skids blindly into the intersection, stopping dead.

In a gleaming-cherry convertible, girls, drunk and wild, wheel up to the curb near him. Alex attacks, yelling as he pursues them into the driveway.

The browned girls sweetly call out, "Hi, Alex!"

He slides to stop at their car door, his toy front tire banging theirs. He grins at these near-naked women whose breasts present themselves as something he wants to see.

"Wa-want to see me-see me…"

"Hey, Alex," the muscled male behind the wheel says. "You want a car like this someday, when you're big like me." Beach Bod turns to the women, grinning.

Little Alex stays quiet, kicking gravel, rocking his bike, and turning the wheel from side to side.

"Yeah and…"

The honey-hued driver laughs, the others laugh, someone hops from the car, and another comes from the house. Cigarettes burn, a song plays, a pint of gas vaporizes. Then another car arrives, and more girls say, "Hi Alex," and snicker and change seats. In a commotion of slammed doors and slung gravel and joyous horns, the driveway clears out, and little Alex watches, abandoned.

Of course, he chases whichever car to the corner, shouting, grinning, bent over the baby handlebars. He pumps the pedals madly, his banged blond hair blown apart in the center. Older faces watch from the 200-year-old windows on the street, observing a small boy forgotten.

"That little brat is going to get hurt out there," one says.

Alex evokes pity and scorn, for no one really expects him to grow up to be normal.

When the intersection quiets, Alex scoffs at the silence expanding and closing around him.

"Wh-where is you going? he shouts, rolling his head for thrust.

He drifts his bike into the intersection where a car hurrying downhill slows and toot-toots, as if trying to tickle this little boy with a cute sound.

"You-you get out of the way!" he sasses.

With the bouncy-boned buoyancy of a little boy, he churns the pedals of the bike uphill. Then, he coasts back onto his safe, dull street with hatefully harsh grunts, guttural and clangorous enough to trigger from him, "What the hell is that?"

His mother, presumably, appears on a plain pine balcony above him, darkly shadowed by the building across the street.

"Get in the driveway, Alex!"

Her appearance and manner show her to be a local with a booming, mannish voice. When she walks away from him, he retorts, in clear stutters, "You g-get in the driveway, woman."

Her intrusions always upset him and drive him farther down the street. He aims his front tire over a curb, around a sewer grate, and crashes through heavy gravel. He hums to himself while the street sparkles with a Colonial maritime charm—white eaves, Gothic towers, varnished clapboards, and elaborately pitched roofs pressed up into a leafy canopy spotted with sun drops.

Lonely, Alex slows to a continuous drift, his bare feet off the pedals. He mumbles to himself, finding a way to reflect his voice to a little ghost friend his age.

Something on the walk catches his eye—a bug scrambling from the rolling shadow of his tire. While he wonders whether to crush it, the radiating spokes of his wheel amaze him as they turn and carry him forward.

His mother calls for him again. Mutilated speech sputters from his small, angry mouth, in a spray of blunt and sharp sounds. He chomps and spits sounds at her, undecipherable pronunciations so spewed and epileptic in rhythm that he makes himself hideous even though only a little boy.

"A car hit-t me! Woman, a car hit me!"

Or he rolls down the sidewalk, out of her view, humming to himself again. Standing on the pedals, hopping the curb, and zipping into the quiet, shaded intersection, looking neither way.

Someone in a window above calls to him.

"Watch out for cars!"

"You!" he immediately challenges, not looking up, "Wa-atch out for cars."

He sounds surprisingly determined, sure of the contempt he feels towards this voice issuing an order. Yesterday, though, he smiled and giggled when he heard a similar warning.

Distracted by his whirling green spokes, he remains in the crossroads, coasting in a circle. When the voice calls to him again, little Alex glares up at the window, lunging his head as he shouts, quite clearly, "Shut u-up or I'll kick your a-ass!"

He darts back onto his street, brakes, and drops his bike to grab a stick on the walk. He jabs the stick into the brush, growling, "I hate you stupid cat...I hate you."

Drugs come to mind, drugs in the bodies of his parents when bearing him. Up close, he shows a Cro-Magnon–like jaw and high protruding lips. The physical blemishes—welts, scratches, and bruises—mark every hostile whoop he asserts and every daredevil swerve and skid he risks.

Through the hazy panes of the yellow apartment, he looks below so charmingly disobedient, a fitful boy, small and inquisitive from the high windows.

"Don't run into the street, Alex," he hears again.

Being corrected bothers him, so he rocks his bike, readying to race away. Unnatural baby fat hangs from his limbs and chest, and his chest is full of dents and creases, the kind of ruddy flesh on a chubby, settling body.

"But why?"

He grins now, showing small, dirty teeth, jagged and neglected.

"Because cars can hurt you."

"But why?"

Again, he grins, his mouth and jaw repulsive.

"Because they're big and heavy and—"

"But why?"

"Well…"

"But why?" he chimes automatically.

Brain damage comes to mind, too. His parents smoked or injected before blundering in bed. His chemical-caused handicap wells in his small, sunstruck eyes as the epitome of an inhuman crime afflicting his damaged body. So where are his inhuman parents? Is his mother above?

"Where is you going?" he asks instinctively, to stop his own neglect.

"Away."

"But why?"

The damage proves overwhelming and irreparable. Forever marred by his creators, Alex becomes a kind of centaur, half beautiful child, half ugly adult, a creature itself a race.

# Silver Balloons

I remember when I first spoke, when my jaws frayed and snapped the fierce wires of my six-year silence. Sounds of speech cracked from my mouth. I spoke not perfectly, not easily, and not sensibly. In fact, I stammered and giggled to the cabby who, growing concerned as I yammered about my sickness, hurried me to the psychiatric clinic. He undercharged me in sympathy. I rambled confessions to scads of phone counselors without last names. Flighty and manic, I behaved erratically in support groups for depression. In my search for employment, I overtalked in interviews, blowing bubbles of pointless yak. I confessed to anyone who'd listen that for six years, I was silent, invisible, and forgotten.

In Massachusetts, at my sickest, I feared that if I were to speak outdoors in unedited phrases, my idiomatic choices of prepositions and my imperfectly rhythmic syntaxes would rise like silver helium balloons out of my grasp. Unfit for heaven, they'd twist and turn in the sky forever as suffering souls.

"That's freakin' nuts!" my friend Gary says, sitting at my kitchen table.

I like Gary a lot. Every time I look at him, he reminds me of Gary Cooper in a defiant role. He's much taller than I am, and in this additional height, he rises to a duty to watch over me.

I continue my story. In how I talked, I must outdo the artful writer John Updike in how he wrote. Gary leans forward and descends on my face.

"Who in the hell is John Updike?"

He really doesn't know, and that's the beauty of it.

Updike was the hero of my arrogance. I was 26, not long out of college. I had already achieved some success by emulating Updike's writing style and epiphanic short stories. Though, my publishers were small and unknown. Also, I was recently married and earning nothing as a writer while living in a grouchy New England town where my manner of work was viewed as loafing. I resented my wife's parents for their working-stiff mentality. Get a real job, they said. You can't make no living putting words down on paper.

When these plebians spoke, English exploded into a deadly shrapnel of solecisms. My wife at the time, by speaking for me, threw herself on these grenades. The sky over her, not over me, was filling with balloons of blunders in speech. Better her soul than mine, I thought.

Then something happened. I got quiet.

"You took yourself out of the world in spite," Gary figures.

"In spite?" I play back to him. "No, in shame."

I won't replay the American sob story. Everyone feels pain, and everyone's pain is unbearable. In my case, my ego was big, but my self-esteem was small. One of my legs was shorter than the other, yet I expected it to keep up. In one hand, I fisted a battered sledgehammer, and in the other, I held a silk handkerchief for my tears.

"Shame," I say, "and…dishonor."

At the newspaper where I worked, I wrote to impress, not to inform. Not what I said, but how I said it mattered only. The sky was not blue, but azure. In language, I took on a pretentious crusade built on unworkable beliefs.

In short, my bad ending, I tell Gary, resulted from vanity and self-criticism. Specifically, I insisted on speaking both extemporaneously and perfectly. But when spoken spontaneously, my words pop, ping, screech, and thunder off the tracks like boxcars. For years, I berated myself. I hammered my knees. I must! I must! I must speak as well as I write! Again and again, I beat myself black and azure.

Writing, composed and harmonized, was music, a grand melody of tunes and notes. It was also an exact science of thoughts. Science and art. Sentences, when spoken as well as written, embodied in my mind gilded Victorian sculptures.

"A conceit above God" was how one counselor described it.

I was grammar obsessed, he told me.

"Grammar-obsessed," I corrected.

Gary's story as a drunken postal worker spins on the wheel. Self-punishment. He may be from Wisconsin, but Wisconsin might as well be West Virginia. I could have his arrest record, and he could have my psychological profile. Regret is what we have in common.

"But whatever you've done wrong," he often says today. "You shouldn't beat yourself black and blue."

Sure. Got it. No question. What matters today is what we call "self-care."

So, after two years, I am speaking naturally. I am flippant as well as professorial. I drivel. I confuse. I mishandle big words. I shout in the open air. I listen to Gary talk about his AA meetings, and he listens to me ruminate myself into a literary fugue. Talk. It is a lovely sound, full of imperfections, beautiful imperfections. Today, there are no silver balloons above me.

"Who in the hell is John Updike?" I laugh.

# Fourteen Seconds

I will start and, I fear, end our story with my mother-in-law, the badgerer. On Monday afternoon, the nervous woman, having heard about John-John's disappearance, called her daughter at work. Nicole worked for John-John's magazine *George*.

"I could hear it in her voice," Nicole fumed to me after she got home, waving her hands hysterically to mimic her mother. "Now ya see that? He took a risk. I told you. See what happens when you take stupid risks?"

Why was he flying at night? Why couldn't he have just driven there? What was he doing up there in the first place?"

John F. Kennedy, Jr., as a relatively new pilot, was not yet instrument-rated, meaning that he could not fly solely by instruments. So, to orient himself, he needed to see where the sky met the land. On the evening he disappeared, haze obscured the land.

Coincidentally, around 9:30 in the evening when his aircraft disappeared off radar, Nicole and I had been standing, we both remembered now, on the patio of the Ocean Edge Resort overlooking the ocean—ocean that turned into liquid concrete under him when his plane crashed some miles north of Montauk Point, Long Island. I even recalled that, while we sipped wine and gazed through the evening sky at the sea, I spoke philosophically at the very time of his crash, posing the question of whether the ocean impeded the reach of the land or did the land block the passage of the sea? Which separated which?

We chuckled at the puzzle of point of view, while offshore, Kennedy's plane smacked the sea, blew apart, and the debris sank down a hundred feet.

"You're right, Mother," Nicole conceded on Monday afternoon. "More and more I'm thinking it's something he did wrong."

"Why? He was perfectly capable. But he took a risk."

"Mom, life is about risks. Starts with being born."

"Honey, look at her father. He's the age he is because he exercised caution…"

On that fateful Friday evening at the resort, at the Overland Café, Nicole announced a surprise for me. She reached for her purse.

"I made you a key for our apartment."

My eyes showed delight. We were not living together yet, but I was regularly staying overnight at her grand East End apartment overlooking the East River.

She extended her arm to an elegant reach and handed me the key.

"I want to give this a try, Mark."

Then, just seconds after entrusting me with the key to her apartment, she mentioned her friend John-John again.

"My brother really liked him."

I threw her a skeptical look. Her short, balding, Jewish brother would admire any all-American boy.

"…thought the same of him as I did," she went on. "Just a regular guy…."

Trust fund. Private airplane. Limo to work. Regular guy? Did she have a thing for him? I asked her outright.

"Every woman does!" she laughed.

For my sore look, she hardened her attitude.

"Well, let me ask you something then. Do you like to see rich people suffer?"

I felt her disenchantment with me. My answer was yes, but I could not free the word across the threshold of my pure mouth. Even though I had never met him, John-John's death quite satisfied me. It seemed an act of fairness.

"You know, Mark," she added. "They've found the second headrest."

I felt an eyebrow raise. The hope that he might somehow still be alive, castaway on a rock or washed ashore still clinging to debris, had lingered until now. Finding one headrest clinched that his whole plane had obliterated.

"So he's dead," Nicole concluded, having informed me of this latest news. "And you're glad, aren't you?"

I defended myself, but not very convincingly.

What I envied about sporto John-John was not certainly his high-adventure tragic death, but rather his glamorous, privileged, exceptional life. Though we were nearly the same age, the President's son had inherited a Fifth Avenue childhood and Ivy League education, all while beautiful women availed themselves to him for his looks, class, prestige, and power. To the opposite extreme, I had started life in the dirt of Appalachia. Redneck brother, jailed father, whorish sister, mental mother, all in smelly Adamsville, Kentucky, where coal dust covered the windows of the school buses.

John-John killed? Good. He had enjoyed enough of life.

But his death grew into an issue between Nicole and me that we could not settle, a dispute we could not resolve. What embittered me, according to her, was that I could not choose for myself a childhood like his. Worse, I wouldn't admit that, by all accounts, the celebrity son of the President was a likeable, regular guy.

Nicole alarmed me. Why, I wondered, was she so susceptible to the gloom of his death? The world had known of John-John's disappearance for almost a full day now. We also knew that, in all likelihood, he had been sitting, strapped in his cockpit, on the floor of the ocean since Friday, three days ago. But Nicole, not I, imagined her John-John drifting through the sea, his face bronzy in the moonlight, and he was smiling at her.

She missed him, his perfect face, his sweet ease with people, but at the same time, she felt confused by her own grief, unsure of its realness, as if her feeling of loss were deceiving her. Furthermore, in comparing her life to John-John's, to the risks and enjoyment she never experienced, she felt even admiration for his death. The seething ocean that refused to release his body to the surface had ultimately granted him the last great word on life—gusto!

He was the poster boy for Camelot. So what would it have served him if he hadn't lived life to the fullest? Nicole now needed to know. She looked up at me.

"I haven't done that yet, Mark."

For the first time, Nicole was dealing with sudden death, her therapist told her. On that ordinary Friday afternoon, she nearly stopped John-John in the hallway of the magazine. "Ah, I don't want to bother him now," she said to herself. "I'll do it Monday.

So she waved goodbye to John-John in the hall for the weekend, and now—poof!—she'd never see him again. One unremarkable moment with him became her last.

On Monday, the Coast Guard was still searching for his plane. Radar indicated that it hit the north Atlantic seven miles off Martha's Vineyard. Found were pieces of luggage, and another headrest had washed ashore overnight. Aviation experts, in revising this calculation of rate of descent of his plane, reduced the length of time of the fall from over a minute to just fourteen seconds.

"Fourteen seconds? That's all?" Nicole sounded angered. John-John deserved more time to solve his problem, more time to live.

In her grief, she toyed with her Ebel sports watch. John-John wore the same watch. His had been scratched up by outdoor play: rugby in Central Park, rock climbing in the Berkshires, jet-skiing up the East River. Anne's watch still looked brand new, cowardly brand new: unscratched, unnicked, entirely unchallenged.

As she gazed at the endless continuation of the second hand, she counted, then recounted, fourteen seconds. She imagined John-John's plane dropping 1500 feet before breaking up in the black sea. She pictured the savage currents, the white debris. Water, at his rate of descent, must have flattened him like a wall.

Fourteen seconds to live. She often counted them, hearing them echo like tolls of a solemn bell and feeling the time pass through her like a chant.

One.

The plane coughed and lurched downward. John-John felt the sudden, sickening plunge.

Two.

Horror grew into an octopus of hysteria as the plane whined downward. Panic, paralysis, prayers.

Three.

Flailing passengers, his wife and her sister, clawed at the inside of the plane.

Four.

Nicole brought herself awake. What matter had she wanted to discuss with John-John on Monday?

She moped all evening. "Maybe he shouldn't have been up that night. He might not have crashed the next day." Or maybe he had been overconfident, her sensible voice said, overconfident in believing in his own invincibility.

Nicole lay on the sofa, moping. John-John excited people, and they remarked about him. Of course, he injured himself from time to time, breaking an ankle, bruising a forearm, but he neither avoided nor invited danger. He hang-glided, surfed, and rollerbladed, simply because adventure gave him keen satisfaction.

She imagined John-John once again as his plane stalled and spun, then nose-dived into the black sea. Did he, in those final seconds, regret the risk?

"Oh, John-John," she sighed with a faint, unlived smile. "You silly boy."

On the morning after the crash, which still remained unknown to us at the time, while Nicole and I were tossing a Frisbee on the beach, helicopters buzzed low up the shore, looking, we presumed, for a lost boater. I felt concern, I remember, for this poor anonymous person in peril at sea.

"Eerie," I said, staring at those black dragonflies along the horizon.

Meanwhile, Nicole asked our elderly neighbor on the private beach to take our picture. We were an attractive couple, he said with a smile. We beamed. We worried that we looked ridiculous together, that we caused a visual discord, she 48 and I 36, leaving 12 years of contrast. But it seemed we were fooling the world. Only Nicole knew that under my curly top I was balding and that behind my front caps, my molars were crumbling. I knew her tricks, too: hair color, sunglasses, loose shorts.

In the late afternoon as we were traipsing up the beach path that wound between the dunes, heading back to the resort, she stopped where the sand thinned at the roadway.

"My sandals," she requested, sitting on a bench.

I produced them from my gym bag and knelt to put them on her, my Cinderella, scrawny, shy, and unpopular as a child. Nicole was pretty, and she was a Jew. So in New York, she was immune to bad luck and unhappiness. Still, a wicked force troubled her life. She would later name it anxiety.

Nicole grew desperate for the contentment of vigorous experiences. We should buy a sport utility vehicle, she suggested, and redecorate the living room in white leather. John-John's death had aroused her conscious interest in an exciting life, but fear and small-mindedness still overcame her at times, in insidious relapses.

Earlier the other morning, for example, as a result of my running the vacuum cleaner while she was blow-drying her hair, a fuse blew, the apartment went dark, and my darling went berserk. She bounded out of the bathroom, naked, dripping-wet, and nasty.

"What have you done to my apartment!"

We located the fuse box in the hallway, opened it, and stood perplexed by the switches. All the while, Nicole was growing more upset, and I more and more apologetic.

She whimpered to me, "Oh, honey, what have you done?"

I turned to her. She looked terrified, drawn in fright, desperate to control this chaos, in this place where she had lived for twenty-eight years in quiet and calm and regularity. Such overreacting, ironically, was how Nicole often described her mother's behavior.

With power restored, the electric alarm clock was blinking, the TV hissing static, and the answering machine resetting.

"God, everything's changed!" she cried out.

I felt himself detaching, withdrawing from her. I stood calmly by myself, aloof and utterly indifferent to her panic.

Worse, the night passed restlessly, our minds rioting in wild dreams, our snores bursting each other awake. In the morning, Nicole felt a gruesome mix of fatigue and panic, her mind slow but her movements fast. She fussed with the alarm clock, then hurried to check the answering machine, a six-figure advertising exec in a tizzy because of a blown fuse.

The sudden awareness of living thirty years in one place petrified her. The interior of her apartment looked nailed down: every chair, pillow, and spoon straightened, every poor thing in proper place, life labeled, all confusion eliminated. Nicole, in this way, had methodized every aspect of daily life: trash to the door after breakfast, Metro Card in hand two blocks before her stop, and five Snackwell cookies after her workout. Life by taxonomic classification.

Another time, while we were walking on 1st Avenue, at 68th Street, she discovered that her favorite card shop had closed at some indefinite, though recent, time. She panicked. Rainbow Cards, in operation since she had moved to the neighborhood more than twenty years ago, had suddenly closed. Why? God, where did it go? Part of her childhood vanished before her eyes. She looked to me for help.

To heaven, along with people and things like spark plugs and salamanders, I thought. I was not mocking her, but her seemingly trivial concern did annoy me. I liked the sophisticated, worldly Nicole, the department head with a stately Manhattan apartment. The closing of a card shop—why was she so alarmed?

By Tuesday midday, we were back in the city. The deputy editor was boxing up John's belongings. A company meeting would take place later today. Flowers were arriving.

At home, Nicole's mother was visiting. I introduced myself politely and moved on, politely. Instantly gone were her daughter's poise and composure. Again and again, into a bicker they flew, one arguing, the other maneuvering out of the way, all while I eavesdropped from the kitchen. In the shadow of JFK Jr.'s death, I was a letdown as a son-in-law.

"No, he's not Jewish, Mom!"

There was a quiver, a flicker, to Nicole's words, even verging on a quarrel. She grew louder and louder, yelling down the old nag.

"What does that matter to you?"

Nicole was punching well, I could hear, but the petulant old broad wrangled back, and both women heated up in a dispute over me, both fanning a controversy: Nicole in a relationship with a gentile.

"Is he rich?"

No? Oh, good heavens!

Nicole's mother exhibited unrelenting nervous energy, a woman always noisy, excited, and declamatory, always clawing at the world, antagonist to all, the tireless belligerent. She sparked and popped in a perpetual state of combustion.

"When will I meet her?" I had teased for weeks.

"Never!" her daughter snapped.

"I want to meet her," I announced.

Nicole, sitting at the kitchen table and leafing through a J. Crew catalog, cast me a scrunched-up look of disbelief.

"You will not!"

If only I had not.

A week after the accident, the Coast Guard hauled John-John's body up from the ocean floor. The bodies of his wife and her sister, divers found shortly later under debris. All three dead, all three lost.

Nicole did not comment further. She was flying on, making an airshow of her feelings for her future. In her mind, she criss-crossed the world, hiking across Italy, watching the painters in the Parisian subways, sampling Ireland.

We adopted a new motto and promise not to become accomplices in small fears, small personalities, small days. We must strive to grow, develop, and extend our relationship.

"Let's drive down," Nicole suggested.

"Where?"

"To Kentucky." Her voice slurred from the wine. "I'm serious, hon. We need to keep on risking it."

So we drove down to Kentucky, through the Blue Ridge Mountains, the weekend, the weather, the roads, all ideal.

"Well, this is Adamsville," I announced on the second day.

In the sunny afternoon, Nicole sat up, then she sat up further.

"Honey, this is suburban."

Suburban? I looked ahead. The Pizza Hut, World Cineplex, and Pier 1 Imports had stood here when I was a boy. That is, the previous businesses in these same buildings—Red Barn, Tower Records, Waldenbooks, etc. These shopping malls had lasted and expanded through my lifetime, running straight through Adamsville, feeding the region with the American charm: the mall-based service economy. Office parks, gas plazas, and a concrete causeway of interchanges, all stretched to the west, within commuting distance of the state capital.

Nicole was right. I had grown up in the suburbs. My hometown was not Appalachian, as I told everyone for years.

"Honey," she went on. "This is middle class."

She left me dumbfounded. I was not underprivileged in my youth. I was all-American.

She leaned forward to read signs for Maplewood Executive Homes, Garden Terrace Place, and Greenbush Estates.

"Honey, you grew up in a nice area."

I eased off the accelerator. All of my life, I had regarded myself as a boy from Appalachia.

"Honey," she broke in. "Don't we want 9C?"

My mind, my purpose for returning to my hometown, proved so disturbed by my new awareness of this region as suburban, not rural, that I widely missed my exit. How had I failed to differentiate where I was raised from where my ancestors had settled? Why, more to the point, had my hometown become in my mind indistinguishable from the Appalachia my parent's parents had endured and often recollected? How could I have confused my heritage with theirs?

"It's okay, hon. We can just take I-7 to Coverton."

I looked over at Nicole who was fingering through Google Maps. Even in my little blue car, which had no radio or air-conditioning, she carried the look of wealth. Her auburn hair, frizzed by the hot air off the highway, shagged down over her jeweled ears.

"Or we could even take Jackson Parkway over to Rochester. Or even Mill Road to…looks like Route 2. That would probably be the most scenic."

I was not responding, but staring straight ahead, my mind a jumble of dark amazement. How had I deluded myself? I was no poor child of this region. My father, in the late 70's, had earned nearly $40,000 a year at the East Kingston Transfer Station. My family was not poor. I was not an Appalachian. I was a middle-class child who had satisfactorily attended public schools.

"Or Valley Road to I-3. Any of these."

Nicole was a researcher, a problem solver. For her, things have to make sense, things sharply divided into right and wrong, things proper and improper, things controlled and out of control. To solve was to control, and to organize was to survive.

Her therapist, Dr. Lowenstein, challenged her to solve the equation: Nicole = x.

Nicole answered: Nicole = Mark (or y) or John F. Kennedy, Jr.

What she liked most about John-John was that even though important and well-off, he remained unaffected and not necessarily elegant. To this point, she recalled when, on an especially cold December day, he wore earflaps to work—green earflaps with a suit.

"Now that took guts!" she declared in his honor.

All the way from Delaware, she had held her iPhone on her lap. Riding with her, I wondered whether John-John's wife, onboard his fated plane, had been as helpful as Nicole was now, whether she had helped him fly from place to place.

"Or we can keep going to Sullivan Dam Road."

How could I have misidentified all of this?

"You're right, it's not a poor area," I said.

She laughed. "You grew up in a nicer area than I did."

* * *

"Darling, aren't you going to introduce us?"

Nicole emerged from the kitchen, looking argumentative.

"Mother, you know him already!" she snapped. "He said hello at the door."

"Well, I know, dear, but he didn't say who he was."

Nicole turned to me to put an end to this matter at once.

"Mark, this is my mother." She then turned to her mother. "Mother, Mark."

We smiled at each other, Mother Russia and Johnny Rotten.

Nicole stepped back into the kitchen, so I turned to Mrs. Newman but remained strangely quiet. Meanwhile, in the parlor, Nicole's brother and her father were arguing about the quickest route here from the Upper West Side.

Throughout dinner, Mrs. Newman was infected with an angry strain of anxiety. Harry, nagged and dominated by his wife for more than half a century, obeyed her yet again, hoisting his old clacky bones into action by poling his dead, skinny legs upright. But when he stood shakily to reach across the table for the massive tray of potatoes, Nicole popped up and carried the hefty brick around the table to him.

Her mother looked upset.

"What in the world, dear. Oh, Nicole, you didn't have to get up."

"Well, mother," the younger woman answered back, straining to lower the heavy dish. "Neither did he."

Mrs. Newman was dumbfounded by her daughter's impertinence.

"Well, he was closer, dear."

"But you don't have to bother him for that, mother."

Harry, I should add, was the typical ethnic New York Harry, a small man attached to his wife like a terrier whose only rebellion consisted of a yip and a wag.

Mrs. Newman, with the bulbous black eyes, glared at her daughter, appalled by her sass. But Nicole was not yielding. Meanwhile, hunchbacked Mr. Newman, pathetic in his withered dependent manner, raised his head as if for the last time.

"Burying me already?" he croaked, in a half-hearted, smiling complaint.

The old soul, with his watery red eyes, looked to me for sympathy—but I didn't risk it. Silence was the only safe place.

But I goofed in another manner. When I pushed my plate aside, Mrs. Newman clasped me in her vision, the long glints of her eyes like claws.

"What?" she exclaimed, horrified by my rejection of her buttered meatballs. 'You don't like them?"

Around the table, all quieted and turned to me, and pressure built in my head. The newcomer, the gentile from Appalachia, was at immediate risk of losing favor with the mother. I felt the heat of embarrassment smear colors across my face, first yellow, then black, then red, until I was the color of mud.

"Mother," protested Nicole. "He doesn't have to eat them."
I was grateful for the intervention.
Meanwhile, the son, the favorite in every Jewish family and often the leader, was leaving me alone, in decided non-interference I both appreciated and respected. Then, in a move that dared objection and even comment, Nicole stood, rounded the table past her mother, then her father, and sat cozily beside her brother. The two of them murmured between them, laughed, then, in high-spirited, childlike mischief, giggled at their parents.

What a ridiculous family! What a strange dance, how they related, everyone at first ornery, then everyone silly. All their anger for one another now seemed phony.

Chatter once again gathered into an argument, with Nicole reminding her father that he lost his hair more than just a few years ago while her brother corrected their mother by pointing out that sugar, even if deleterious to the diet of children, was nonetheless a highly lucrative, global cash crop.

On this subject, I thought Ira spoke out of his area of expertise. He was a private attorney who, as a matter of practice, defended tenants in dispute with landlords. But for all his integrity and compassion, his business was failing. Rumor in the family told of his routine financial dependency on his mother, and this indebtedness to her left him both beholden and ashamed, to say nothing of further irresponsible in matters of money. For his predicament, Nicole both pitied and scorned him, feeling sorrow for his disgrace yet, at the same time, resenting the favoritism shown to him. To comfort himself, he overate. He was obese, tripled-chinned and bald.

To me, the father was a disgrace, a scrawny, henpecked half-a-man, badgered and beaten—"Harry, do this! Harry, do that!"

"Daddy, why do you put up with it?" Nicole once pleaded to know, to reach him, to urge him to respect himself.

But her father brushed off her unnecessary concern with a laugh.

"Oh, I'll get back at your mother," he promised.

Retaliate he did—by depriving her of a successful, presentable husband.

What Nicole remembered of her father was a small-shouldered man so unfortunate in the family business that he borrowed her weekly allowance, which came from her mother, then her babysitting money, which came from neighbors. What she remembered of her mother was stinginess. She would never become like her father. She had all of New York City, 2,000 city blocks, in which to make her money.

Throughout dinner, the more Mrs. Newman observed me, the more she badgered her husband. He couldn't even find the highway south, she accused the scrawny 81-year-old man over matzo balls.

I studied him. He seemed an incurious creature, a man who preferred to be an obedient boy, an old child. So bullied was he that he smiled feebly as she punched him once more with disrespect. For half a century, their marriage practiced this art of attack and defense, of returning like for like, of repaying emotional injuries. I worried what influence the mother's ill treatment of her husband and his grueling submissiveness had on my Nicole.

Her mother, through dessert, seemed a woman having daggers constantly thrown at her, and, with this rain of blades around her, she endangered anyone near her. Her every breath seemed a gasp of alarm or a sign of woe. As her reluctant daughter, Nicole regarded their common biology as a terribly unfair contamination. She was, to Nicole, in one cruel word, an embarrassment.

Then, in an explosion of voices that sounded like gulls roosting, everyone argued: mother, father, daughter, son, all yakking at one another. These were the Newmans, a foursome rife with conflict, parents and children quick to quarrel, a family disposed to disagree yet somehow content to contend. They sat on the sofa and argued, they ate at the table and argued, then they sat on the sofa again and argued some more. They spoke the English of naggers and criticizers and arguers, clanking heavy iron swords of emotion, eyes quivering and flickering. Men, their pitches heated, disagreed on which and when certain New York avenues were passable—knowledge of the city in this respect proved important—and women, their noisy voices antagonized one another with feelings and opinions kept hidden. Good health was celebrated by active quarreling.

"I did it!" Nicole exclaimed, calling me in the middle of a Tuesday. "I booked us for two weeks in Italy!"

We would join a hiking group in Pisa, then continue to Sienna, by way of trails past vineyards and Etruscan ruins. We would explore caves and tombs, picnic alongside olive gardens, stay in charming inns, trek through oak forests, tour cobblestone villages, and even spectate a wild, barebacked horserace.

I listened, struck dumb by the excitement awaiting us.

"Just the kind of trip John-John would have taken," I remarked.

Nicole paused, then whispered to me, "I want us to live."

# The Spirit in My Shoes

In my dark life after divorce, my spirit lives in my shoes.

Let's start with boots. Whether bulky and cloddish or stylish and smart, boots grasp my ankles like strong hands and hold me to the earth, my spirit grounded. I'm heavy and somber. I plod like a farmer in the marsh, even in sporty, compact, low-top boots. In my bad marriage, by the way, I wore steel-toed boots to bed.

Looking for salvation, I try insulated casual shoes. At first, I strut and flounce with a flamboyant personality. I love their sturdy outer covering, along with the empowering height of their thick soles, all with a dressy façade. But as high-tops, casual shoes press against my veiny ankles and disrupt circulation. Walking is painful. Friends say I look dismal and burdened.

Incidentally, sneakers are not a serious shoe.

This evening, while strolling in my new penny loafers, I arrive in the past, in my carefree late teens. I feel young again. Rosewater splashes me. Horns blow. Cars stop. I bebop with the vigor of a positive heart. My hermitage has not permanently deformed me. My spirit did not rupture and deflate, sinking me into old age. Instead, I am a curmudgeon decompressed. In these pliant shoes, these sponges of delight, my heel meets the earth with soft acceptance. My foot is bendable, and my body formative. I yield to barriers.

Beautiful women passing in dark suits raise their large, dripping-wet eyes at me. I am a handsome man in a Dockers commercial. All the while, under me, my toes wiggle the whole planet. I pause to look down at my supple-dupple shoes. Then I skip. I shuffle. I twirl a whole city block.

My shoes! They are my stepping stones to happiness.

As I stride across the wide, busy street, I am jumping on a pogo stick. Eyes, tinted with the electric-red of taillights, follow me. I am desirable. I am free—free from these dark days after divorce to vault over the world and make rainbows with my good intentions.

I gaze up at the cloudy evening sky orange from the lighted towers of the city. In my stargazing stupor, I do not see the punks veering toward me.

"Hey, little man, you stoned or somethin'?" one snarls.

I do not respond. He's wearing sneakers.

# Vineyards In a Far-Off Land

On our way back from town, Mom and I spotted Ernesto, the new artist in Harpers Ferry, walking along the highway. We shot past, and I begged her to stop. She looked at me as if for the life of her she couldn't understand me. Then, she took her foot off the gas and began signaling over.

"I don't know about this, Josh," she said.

I stuck my head out the window and peered back down the highway. Ernesto was trying to catch up, but the large sheets of paper he was gripping in one hand bent in the wind and slowed him down. I told Mom to back the car up, but she said that was too dangerous to do on the shoulder.

He reached us at last.

"Josh?" he said, smiling.

He knew me from the streets of Harpers Ferry, where I was always following the artists around. Then he looked in at my mother and I turned and watched her look at him for the first time.

Nothing big happened. She was pleasant, and he was pleasant.

He had difficulty fitting the paper into the backseat, so my mother offered to open the trunk. But he solved the problem by bowing the paper until it fit between the seats. Then he squeezed himself in the side, and Mom pulled away as if we were now hauling something fragile.

Everyone was quiet at first. I looked back. He had that same warm smile and tanned face under white stubble.

"It is nice of you, Josh," he said, "to have your mother stop."

His accent. It always made me think of someplace far away, and that was strange, imagining a faraway place in our old West Virginia car.

"Were you just back at Merimack's?" my mother asked, glancing in the mirror.

I was turned around in the seat, so that I could watch both him and Mom without moving.

He said he must confess that he did not know what Merimack's was.

"Our office supply in town?"

"Yes, of course," he said, smiling.

I saw a gold tooth in the corner of his mouth. He said something else, but it was lost in the sound of air coming in the window, which Mom would wind up a little.

"They have a nice selection there, don't they?" she said. "My son gets all his art supplies there."

"Yes, Josh likes art," he said. "That is very good, Josh. You must show me your work sometime."

I kept looking at him. His voice was full of strange, beautiful sounds.

"Josh has always had an interest in drawing," Mom said, speaking up toward the mirror as if it were a microphone that went to a speaker in the backseat. "He gets it from his father."

I looked over. Why did she have to say that?

"His father is an artist?" Ernesto asked.

"Well, no, not exactly. He painted some years ago when he was younger."

I thought of my father, not so young anymore, doing nothing with his life.

"My father was also very talented," Ernesto said. "He made little statuettes out of alabaster."

"Oh, you're from Italy then?" Mom asked.

"Yes, Florence."

"Oh, how beautiful."

"You haven't been there?"

"Oh no, but I've seen pictures."

For my mother, pictures were as good as the real thing. She had a coffee table book of Italian pottery, which included the pictures she was talking about.

"This," Ernesto said, looking out the car at the hills outside Charles Town, "reminds me of the northern vineyards in Tuscany."

Mom let her foot off the gas. "This? Jefferson County?"

The only other time she let her foot off the gas was when she remembered something she had forgotten to get at the grocery store for Dad and had to drive back.

"There is a slight resemblance, yes," he said.

Mom looked sick—Jefferson County resembling the beautiful vineyards in some far-off land?

I was surprised she was acting this way. She always said how beautiful our county was and always talked about how awful it was that the Park was taking over all the farmlands. I thought she would like to hear that our county was as beautiful as some far-off place. But she was looking in the mirror at Ernesto as if she didn't need to see the road anymore.

"I was surprised," he said, leaning forward so that we could hear him, "to find out that they have no bus service in this region."

"Oh no, nothing like that," Mom said back, her face full of questions at the same time. "Are you staying here in town?"

"Yes," he said, "at the Hill House. I am with a group of teachers from the Corcoran."

"Oh, the Corcoran Art Institute? I've certainly heard of that."

"Yes, well, we thought the hotel would provide...'shuttle service,' I think it is called. Then I was told it was only a few miles to the town back there." He laughed a little.

"Oh, no," Mom said importantly, "Charles Town is too far to walk. It's a full eight miles."

She was embarrassing with her little facts. So what if it was eight miles? I looked out at the cornfields. Actually, how far it was from Harpers Ferry to Charles Town had been a little matter of dispute in our family. The signs said eight, Dad had said six, our speedometer said five, sometimes seven, but everyone else, including Grandma, thought it was at least ten. And for some reason, the county, when they made this new highway, didn't put in all the mile markers. We settled on eight miles, since Mom couldn't imagine that the county would make such a mistake in math.

"You have been to the Corcoran?" Ernesto asked her.

"Oh, once," she said, "but long ago."

I looked over. "You went?"

"With my mother," she said, not to me but to Ernesto. "But that's been years."

"I was about to ask," he said, leaning forward some more, "do the school children in this region go into the city, to visit the museums?"

"Oh, no," Mom said back, as if he had just asked her something that around here no one ever questioned, like why the liquor stores weren't open on Sunday.

"But why?"

Mom and I looked at each other.

"It seems a short drive to the city."

"Oh no," she said, "it's 65 miles."

That was something else in question. The sign at Harpers Ferry said 65 miles to Washington, D.C., but the one in Charles Town said 76, which couldn't be right if it was eight miles from Harpers Ferry to Charles Town.

Once, we tried to check distance between Harpers Ferry and Charles Town using Mom's wristwatch. My brother Jerry knew from science class that when we are going 60 mph, we were going a mile a minute. So we timed it and ended up with 12 minutes. But that wasn't really accurate either, because half the time Mom was afraid to go to the full five mph over the speed limit, to say nothing of how many times she got stuck behind slow cars. So we settled on 65 miles, just as we had settled on 8 miles, because that's what the sign closest to Harpers Ferry said and because it was the easiest number for everyone to remember, being exactly ten above the speed limit.

But however many miles away the city was, it was not far. If you shut your eyes and counted, it was counting to 60 sixty times. If you went by minutes, it was only a little more than an hour, and a little more than an hour was nothing, just Bewitched and I Dream of Jeannie back-to-back.

"Yes, I suppose it is a long drive," Ernesto said. Only he didn't seem to believe what he was saying.

I looked over at Mom. "It's only an hour." I said.

"Oh, Josh, it's longer than that," she said back.

Mom was thinking back to when the roads between here and there were all twisted up and narrow and you couldn't go fast or pass, when they all had double lines and "Road Narrows" signs everywhere. Today, though, there were brand new car bridges around town and a new highway all the way to Frederick, where there were even bigger roads that led to the city.

This highway we were on was new. Whenever we took it to the shopping mall in Frederick, we saw more and more signs for Washington, D.C., and Baltimore. Mom called it "the metropolitan area." There was a jumble of ramps and overpasses, everything crossing and criss-crossing, somehow coming together, then branching out in every direction. It terrified her.

That was what made it far. Her fear. The city wasn't far for tourists or for anyone not afraid to drive to new places. Dad tried to say that the tires on our car were too old for long trips. But we could have taken the Amtrak to the city or the Greyhound out of Frederick. It wasn't the old tires. It was us.

I looked over at her, determined to win our little argument, even if there was somebody else in the car.

"Dr. Reynolds said it takes an hour," I said. He didn't really say this, but she didn't know."

"Well he probably drives too fast," she said back.

"It takes Mr. Richmond an hour," I said right back.

She gave me an impatient look. "Josh, I know it takes longer. Now stop."

"It took Deedee's father only an hour by Amtrak. A couple of times he even took a bus from Frederick, and that took even less time."

Mom looked in the mirror at Ernesto and said with that kind of smile that only made me madder: "I don't know where my son gets these ideas."

"It's twenty minutes to Frederick, Mom. You said so."

She looked out at the roadway, at the dashes that passed us like milliseconds. She couldn't argue with me about that. We had timed that, too. About twenty minutes for 22 miles, or a mile a minute.

"Well, I guess you're right," she said, because it's another forty miles or so beyond that.

Ernesto leaned forward and said in his thick Italian voice, "As I understand it, the proximity of Harpers Ferry to Washington, D.C., was its value in the Civil War, and that led to the arsenal being erected there."

He sounded as if he had read something from an encyclopedia. Mom didn't know what to say to this.

"What he means, Mom" I said, "is that it was always close."

She gave me a sharp look. But I ignored her, opened that glove box, and took out the Texaco map. I spread the map out on my lap, despite her telling me to put it away because the wind would just blow it around. I knew just where to find Harpers Ferry on it. It was written in italics, as Harpers Ferry Historic National Park, was crowded in by places I had never heard of before, places apparently right beside me all my life. Cumberland Village. New Brighton. Kingston. Route 340 was nothing more than a tiny blue line that went nowhere by itself. It ran into a zillion bigger blue and red lines that twisted around and met with other blue and red lines that came in from everywhere. According to this, the city was all around us. Washington, D.C. was half a pinky away, and the Atlantic Ocean was not much farther. We could see Baltimore, even Philadelphia. I couldn't believe all the thick roads: I-270, 495, 95. On and on. There was this huge, filled-up world all around us that I couldn't see.

Mom went on looking straight ahead. We were coming up on the Harpers Ferry exit. Here the highway seemed especially wide and sunny. I liked the feeling of the world coming here. Around us were trucks from Virginia and Pennsylvania. I even saw a sports car with Delaware plates. Lying along the shoulders were burnt up, fallen-off mufflers and shreds of truck tires, stuff that made the highway seem like a racetrack every car and truck in America was on.

I turned around in the seat.

"What are you gonna draw?" I asked.

He looked at me as if it took a moment to bring his mind back from wherever it was."

"This is for a project I have planned, Josh. A drawing of the Lockwood House."

Mom changed her grip on the steering wheel. "I'm sorry you had to walk so far."

"Oh, I don't mind," Ernesto said. "The countryside here is so beautiful."

She looked up in the mirror. "And you really think West Virginia looks like Tuscany?"

He smiled and nodded, and a few seconds later, I saw Mom look up at a passing sign as if expecting it to read: Tuscany, Next Exit.

# Marshmallow People

They had what they thought was a one-night stand, but when the night became the day, they were still together. Call it a road trip at daybreak.

They pulled off the highway and up to a McDonald's, and while he ran in for Egg McMuffins and sixteen-ounce coffees, she checked her cell, which she had happily turned off last night. It now felt as heavy as a rock with messages—most from her mother. She played the last message first, to cut to the chase, and was relieved to hear nothing but background noise, as her ditzy mother didn't even know how to even leave a message properly.

Soon they were back on 95 South, past Columbia, South Carolina, in the last fifty miles before the Georgia border. The sides of the road were turning swamplike and foul smells were working their way inside the car, even with the windows up. She noticed his unshaven face in the bright sunlight and asked, "How old are you? I never asked."

He looked over with a sly smile that said he had been waiting hundreds of miles to surprise her with the answer.

"Twenty-nine."

"Twenty-nine! No way."

"Yes way."

She sat looking at him wide-eyed, all but letting the car drift.

"Seriously?" she said, her voice going up a pitch.

As easily as he nodded, he nonchalantly looked around his seat, then on the floor.

"Where's the map?" he asked.

Though her snazzy little car was equipped with a voice-activated Heather Quest Navigational System in the dash full of beeping lights and directional arrows, he preferred his old-fashioned Texaco fold-out job. Something else she didn't understand about him, a part-time web designer not liking high-tech equipment.

"You're telling me," she couldn't wait to continue saying, "you're seven years older than I am?"

She sat glancing at him until he finally looked up from his stupid map.

"Yeah," he said, rounding out the word, "and aren't you going to ask me if I'm a deadbeat polygamist dad while you're at it?"

"No, I don't care about that—seven years older, really?"

When he popped out a laugh, she peered across the seat at his face, trying to see these years of difference. She couldn't, just stubble she was starting to wish he'd shave off. So she looked back at the road. Twenty-nine? Which meant he would be thirty soon, maybe as soon as next month, or the month after that.

"Get off at the next exit," he said suddenly.

"What?" she said, looking over.

"The next exit. 17B."

She sat looking at him.

"Go ahead," he said.

Reluctantly, she put on the signal and started exiting under the big shamrock-green sign.

"Burrellville State Hospital?" she said, looking up, then over at him. "Is there something you want to tell me?"

He said nothing until they were nearly to the end of the off-ramp, easing up to a stop sign.

"Turn left."

She did, glancing over at him, then checking the mirror and speeding up. Down an ordinary old county road they went for a few miles, past intersecting roads, drab houses, and a closed-up Bill's Gas.

"Turn up here. Next right," he said, pointing.

"I'm really hoping that you desperately have to use the bathroom here, Thad," she said, signaling and braking, "and you're just being super shy about it."

She glanced over to see him fold up the map, toss it on the dash, sit back, and cross his arms. Not even a smile for her little joke. The road they pulled onto, meanwhile, was curvy and narrower and led past fewer houses.

"Now here," he said, pointing again.

Ahead on the right was a suspicious-looking smaller road entering a heavy overhang of trees.

"Grandview Pike?" she said.

"Turn—don't miss it!"

"OK!"

Grandview Pike was more like Badview Lane—collapsed grain silo, empty logging truck sitting dead along the road, scraggly black dogs around it as if they had eaten both the driver and the logs and were waiting for more.

"Now you do know where you're—"

"Up here," he said. "At the gate."

She slowed in front of a rusted brown sign over a sandy side road.

"West Falmouth Private Cemetery?" she read. "Open till dark?"

She looked over at him.

"OK," she said, bringing the car to a dead stop in the middle of the road. "I need a little more information here."

"Just trust me."

She gave him another long look, shook her head, then eased her new BMW down the rutted, yellow road.

"I guess this is where you kill me, dump my body, and take my car?"

He laughed.

"Yeah," he said.

She looked over.

"Seriously?"

"Just drive. Christ."

She did, over potholes and through low-hanging limbs.

"You know, you could put me at ease by not being so—I don't know—Robert De Niro about this."

He was peering ahead through the thinning evergreens, an eager look on his face. When the cemetery appeared, he leaned forward and gaped around, from his side of the windshield to hers.

"What? They're not keeping it cut anymore?" he cried out, his voice full of outrage, his face full of strain.

"Is a family member buried here? Is that it? Just tell me, Thad!"

He didn't answer, just went on peering around as if he had expected Noah's Ark to be hidden back here in this cemetery and it wasn't.

"A friend? An old girlfriend?" she went on.

"Here."

"What?"

"Stop here!"

She nearly drove up onto a cemetery marker before jerking the car to a stop. The clump of keys in the ignition rapped against the dash as she sat looking over at him.

"You were a murderer in your last job? Is that it?"

"No," he said, opening the door, which donged like a department store elevator as he looked over and smiled, "I made headstones."

Shutting the car off, she hopped out and caught up with him on the drab, weedy grass.

"You made these?" she asked, glancing around at the hard, ugly stones.

He nodded and smiled. But the look on her face was that he was also saying he had landed on the moon and she wasn't believing that either.

"When?" she asked.

"When I lived in Burrellville," he said, smiling, as he went on looking around—twirling around, in fact, like a girl in a field of poppies.

Her arms fell straight by her side.

"You," she said, "lived in Burrellville. These boonies?"

Again, he nodded, all smiles on his little carousel of the moment.

"Right back there?" she said, pointing. "You lived there—when?"

But he didn't answer. Instead, he squatted down in front of a headstone and squinted in close at the lettering, so close he appeared to be using a gem loupe. She heard him sigh.

"Damn."

"What?" she asked.

"I told them so," he said, shaking his head. "Blue Pearl granite chips after a few years." He pointed around at the other headstones nearby. "Sierra White, Paradiso— they're heat-glazed, so they don't." He squinted again at the engraved letters in front of him. "See these tiny cracks?"

But he didn't wait for her to see. Instead, he stepped a few feet over to a traditional gray stone, knelt in front of it, and started running his fingertip up and down the shafts of letters and numbers, across the tops, then following the curves around, as easily as if writing the name of the deceased on the back of a car window. All the while, he had his ear turned to the stone.

She stood, giving him a puzzled grin.

"You look like you're listening for something," she said.

"No, no, I'm feeling." He glanced at her. "Feel how even these are?" he said, a pleased look on his face as he beckoned her over. "That's the trick. Even depth. Straight, square sides. Less erosion."

But he didn't wait for her to feel either. He stood and, bumping into her, stepped back from the gravestone he was all gaga about.

"You take your sandblaster," he said, "put the hose over your shoulder like so—" He pretended to hoist a heavy hose over his shoulder, his hands in a rounded grip. "Then bend at the waist—" He bent. "And, keeping the nozzle plumb to the ground, move the sand spray back and forth across the stone, which of course is placed flat on the ground."

She nodded. Of course.

Then she watched him sway left and right at the hips, bending only at the knees, like a speed skater moving in place, all the while keeping the end of the hose vertical to the ground.

"Just like a machine," he said.

Red-faced in his bent-over position, he made a point of looking back at her as if full well expecting her to take over this piece of equipment after his little demo.

The skill to making good headstones, he went on to say, standing up straight, was not in the sandblasting—that was methodical grunt work—but in stenciling and cutting by hand the rubber template that covered the stone. That, and gluing it to the glazed granite, in particular, tapping it flat with a rubber mallet so that there were no air bubbles to cause it to blow loose during sandblasting, especially around the letter openings. Making the layouts on paper took great care as well.

"Oh, my god," she said, finally stepping up to him, "you really did make these?"

As she stood beaming at him, she saw up close his proud, fatherly look, as if all these stones were his children. "I mean, listen to you," she said.

She reached down, locked her fingers into his, and pulled his hand to her bosom.

"Where's your hard hat, handsome?" she said.

He grinned in a way so effortless, so far from how he ordinarily was.

"I can't believe this," she said, smiling, looking around. "This is so cool!"

Then, letting his hand go, she turned in a complete circle, her arms out like a helicopter blade.

"You made all these?" she asked, pointing across an expanse of hundreds of different headstones: old and new, tall and thin, short and wide, white and dark, a few pink and heart-shaped. "By hand?"

"Oh, no, just the newer ones. Maybe a dozen on this hill," he said.

Then she gave a long look around at the trees that surrounded this remote cemetery, and he told her that the monument company was located just a few miles away, if it was still in business. Eight years ago, when he was here, it was on its last legs. Small and family-owned, it was nothing but a barn with a sand floor, an air compressor, a few slabs of Georgia granite, a shack for storage, and a drafting desk with some rolls of layout paper.

The man who trained Thad also owned the company, but he wanted out. As the last in a family line to run the business, as well as a full-time pharmacy tech in the next town over, he had no interest in making cemetery monuments.

"So why didn't he just groom you to run it?" she asked.

Thad turned to her.

"He did."

"He did?"

There were only three employees back then: Thad, the man's elderly mother, who was the office manager, and an old fellow who hauled the finished stones to area cemeteries.

"Igor?" she said.

Though teasing him, she was absolutely stunned. She sat cross-legged on the grass and looked around at the newer memorials.

"Sarah Jane Pritchard, Born 1943, Died 2003," she said.

When she hopped up to brush a weed off the headstone, she ended up standing and looking down into the frosty, coarse grooves of the letters and numbers. The longer she looked, the more she saw how alone the name looked on the stone by itself, hammered there forever.

"That's it?" she asked, looking back at him. "No husband? No mention of children? Just her?"

She even looked around at her feet as if she had somehow missed a second headstone.

"Was she ever married?" she asked.

She glanced back to see him shrug.

"You mean you never met her?" she asked.

His eyebrows shot up in astonishment.

"Excuse me?" he said, grinning.

She covered her face with her hands.

"Oh, my god, that's so stupid," she said. "I can't believe I just asked that." She laughed, but soon went on looking at the headstone with the same troubled expression.

"Not married," she said. "Probably no children. Alone in the world. And you made her gravestone." She looked over at him. "You were probably the only man in her life."

"The last one for sure," he said.

"Whoa," she said, turning to him, "you have the coolest sense of humor sometimes."

Then she gave the stone another long look.

"What would she say to you now if she could?"

"You spelled my name wrong!" he cried out.

She burst out laughing.

"And you made me too old!" she added.

She stooped and ran her index finger in the same grooves he had, feeling the smooth, even edges he was talking about.

"'Lines on Eternity,'" she said to herself.

"That's called frosting," he said, noticing where her finger had wandered.

Frosting, he explained, was achieved by lightly sandblasting away the granite glaze, making a rough look.

"Like a window?" she asked.

He nodded.

"God, you really made gravestones," she said, shaking her head.

And here she thought all he knew how to do was serve a table of five. That, and complain about chef salads without all the egg picked off.

"Technically, flat and upright markers," he said.

"And you were happy?" she asked, looking up at him. She didn't wait for his answer. "I can see you were—look at your face!" She hopped up and stood close to him. "I don't recognize you. You're glowing." She felt her face. "I'm glowing!"

He tried to downplay it all by saying it was hard, hot work, that you had to wear canvas coveralls and a welding mask, but he only looked all the happier.

"God, this is so cool!" she cried out.

He watched her skip out across the cemetery, touching her hands to the tops of the headstones just as he had before, like Julie Andrews in The Sound of Music.

"You ever use—whatta you call it—a chisel?" she called back. She ran back to him, threw her arms around him, and smiled up into his face. "Like Michelangelo?"

She was a little disappointed when he said no, but it didn't stop her from kissing him.

"They're lovely, Thad. It's like an art."

"Yeah, well, not anymore."

He went on about how the industry was today not only completely automated, but also computerized too. Even relief images, like the praying hands, crosses, and floral designs, were designed by software.

"Order your headstone online today," he said, in a happy, perky voice, "and have it shipped by UPS to your door tomorrow."

She stood smiling at him.

"There's a whole other side to you I don't know." She came up to him. "You're—"

"What?"

But she didn't answer him, not entirely. She instead gave him an inexplicable look, and, from there, they walked down over the hill, through a quiet crowd of short headstones.

"They're like little aliens smiling at us," she said, looking around.

He gave her imaginative thought a smile.

"I can remember doing every stone," he said.

"You remember their names, too?"

"No."

"I can." She stopped and shut her eyes. "Sarah Jane Pritchard. Donald Howard Baker. Betsy W. Baker. Carlin Lee Bell. A. S. Gresham. Perry Davidson II. Emily—somebody."

"Emily Anne Marshall," he said.

"See, you do remember." She gave him an extra look. "God, you're so different suddenly. You look—nineteen. If you shaved, you'd look nine!" She took his hand and pulled him to the ground, where they sat surrounded by his smiling, granite-faced, little alien children. "Wow, this is definitely so permanent," she said. "Just think, your work will be here a hundred years from now."

She looked over at him. She couldn't believe what she was feeling for him. She wanted to make love to him right on the ground, right on top of one of these gravestones. She wanted to grind herself into him, sandblast the letters of her name into his soul.

"How in the world did you ever end up living down here?" she asked. But she didn't wait for the answer. "Better yet, how in the world did you ever end up in Saint Claire?"

They lay back on the grass, looking up at the puffy white clouds drifting over northern Georgia. For the longest time, neither spoke. In the faraway world overhead, she saw, as she always saw when she looked up at clouds, the odd, nonconforming faces of a secret heaven society that didn't exist on earth. When she was a girl, she called the clouds Marshmallow People.

"I was named after my great-aunt Rose—did I tell you?" she asked, looking over at him. "On Daddy's side. She was one-quarter Cherokee." She sat up and pointed to her nose. "That's how I got this nose. It's a Cherokee nose. And this chin. See how far apart my eyes are?"

Looking up at her, he gave a lazy nod.

"See the Indian in me?" she asked, turning to the side. When he nodded too easily, she gave his shoulder a light swat. "Oh, you do not!"

Her great-aunt Rose, she went on to say, lying back on the grass beside him, was a hearty, sturdy woman who worked in the Dryer County cornfields from sunup to sundown, raising eight children.

"With no man around, too," she added. She looked over at him. "And lived to 102."

She could tell he was listening, even if his head was in the clouds.

"Sometimes I feel—and don't laugh—connected to her," she said.

She hoped he would say something, anything, but he didn't. His silent manner had her lunging forward for him, reaching but coming up empty. Eventually, she looked back up at the Marshmallow People.

"I think about her sometimes," she said. "Even see her. Or imagine her in the mirror anyway." She sat up again and nearly peered down into his eyes to get his attention. "I mean, she didn't change the world, but she was hard-working. And long-lived." She glanced around at the cornfield of headstones. "'Great mother nurturer,' is how Daddy describes her."

"Family icon," he said without warning.

"Exactly!"

She was so pleased he said that she sat looking down at him for the longest time, wanting to do something with the moment, to kiss him, to make love to him, or to wait to hear more from him, or even to ask to hear more. The quiet boy had her heart. Eventually, though, she draped her arms over her knees and looked around at the headstones he had made. "I mean, why aren't I good enough the way I am?" she asked. "Maybe God sandblasted my face this way?" She glanced around at the filled-up cemetery. "For eternity."

When she saw him lying with his head suddenly turned to her, his eyes looking up into hers, she knew this was the moment.

"That's why I didn't get this whittled away," she said, tapping her Cherokee nose, "like soap!"

He chuckled a little and looked back up at the clouds.

"But how can I miss my great-aunt when I never even met her?" she went on to ask herself. "She died forty years before I was born." She hoped he would say something about the spirit world, something mystical, Native-esque, but he didn't. So she lay back on the grass beside him, looked up into the endless, indeterminate faces in the sky, gave his hand a squeeze, and said for the two of them, "I'm glad you stayed this morning."

# Renting

What they liked most about the refurbished apartment was its beautifully restored floor-flush fireplace. Framing a blackened brick recess where no evidence of fire remained, the fireplace looked like the façade of a miniature Ionic temple, replete with lifelike entablature, columns, and pedestals, all in handsome white wood. It boasted itself upon the room with stately excellence. The high, sturdy mantel invited pictures and vases. Painted in the same bolting black, the hearth, part brick and part slate, projected itself into the carpeted room as an entranceway before them. She modeled before them, this next hopeful couple.

She was ecstatic. "Oh, honey, isn't it just beautiful!"

But the landlady leading the tour quickly pointed out, "Now it's just for looks. You can't use it."

Her remark seemed minor and failed to disillusion them. Whether functional or ornamental, this atmospheric treasure was theirs.

Earlier that afternoon, when the Wilsons met the owner to present themselves, as coached by their real estate agent, they opened the conservation by praising the old-world charm of the fireplace. They understood, the owner asked, that they could not build a fire in the decommissioned fireplace. Then, in colorful wonder, the wife compared the hearth to a Greek arcade, and its recess to a folk shrine. The owner blinked at her, then noted that while the apartment had stood empty, dust had drifted into the hearth and fire-place. He promised to have it cleaned before they moved in.

He asked, "You have much furniture?"

The couple was mindful of his tactic. He was stalling the moment while his real estate agent stepped into a back room to check their references.

"Oh, no, not much," Debbie promised, interpreting his question as a probe to see if they would trash up the place. "Just the usual things. Sofa, chairs, TV and VCR, desk, microwave"—in her nervousness, she resorted to itemizing their belongings—"and Taffy."

Taffy, a butterscotch tabby kitten, leaped into the moment like the chime of a glass bell.

"Our cat," Mark explained, his jaw clenched.

Out of one side of his mouth, he murmured to himself that the dumb feline was about to kill the arrangement. Their agent, giddy about the prospect of a commission, had assumed that their small pet would pass with the owner. But she forgot to check. The owner, dropping his thin smile, appeared grave. He rubbed his chin. There was a pet fee, he announced, of forty dollars each month.

* * *

As soon as moving into the subdivided Greek Revival home, Mark and Debbie decorated the spaces of their new apart-ment, which had been thoroughly refurbished and even reinvented. The coat closet in the living room was once an old entranceway. The shelves in the anteroom, formerly a closet, spanned to the cabinets in the wraparound kitchen-ette, once a bedroom.

Next came the fireplace. Where to start? In a decorative whim, Deb positioned one of her colored pencil drawings into the opening of the chimney. The edges of the cardboard fit neatly against the tapering brick.

Mark disliked her improvisation.

"Looks goofy."

Taffy, placed on the mantel to stay from underfoot, also looked goofy, peering over the ledge to see what the humans were doing, her stretched neck shortening whenever she lost her balance. Her watery, cartoonish eyes blinked, and when she sniffed, her adorable, damp nose twitched. But meowing earned her a sore look from Mark, still peeved about the increase in rent. Overruled on the matter of the colored pencil drawing, Debbie removed it, pulling it out of the firebox.

"Well, we just can't leave the fireplace like that," she complained. "It's entirely empty."

The void gawked at them. It growled its big black mouth at them. It mocked him.

What will fit in this inglenook other than firewood? What charming adornment will suffice as a modern occupant of this fireplace? Deb and Mark obsessed over it. He hung a eucalyptus wreath. She placed candles. But it proved to be useless and permanent—and they were paying dearly for every inch of the place.

Soon, the high mantel displayed family pictures, seashells, paperweights, and a bowl of fresh pink potpourri. But the space beneath defied them.

"I wish I could just cover it up. Fill it with concrete," he moaned, threatening to ask for a refund in their rent.

She, lenient and persevering, continued to try. A fire extinguisher would certainly fit. Or an antique toddler crib. Maybe a floor fan in the summer. Or the ironing board—or maybe not. Angling a rocking chair in front of the hearth was more a graceless barricade than a décor. Nope, the elaborate fireplace outshone whatever they shoved into it—butler's table, potted plant, even her old Sony stereo with flanking pillar-like speakers.

What they needed, he explained, was a compact item of certain aesthetic value, a porcelain statuette or exotic carving. Frustrated, she threw an armful of velour pillows into the brick recess. Further frustrated, she gathered them up and tossed them onto the sofa.

"Well, what?" she asked.

She knew! She solved the problem by huddling her gang of furry farm animals inside the chimney. Mark, pacing the room, announced his uncompromising skepticism of her using novelties to gag the space.

"Honey, wait!" Buoyantly smiling, she threw her arms up high. "I can't believe I didn't think of it earlier! What about those fake logs and fire?"

After a strong look of consideration, he dismissed the notion as bourgeois—at that very second, while entering the bathroom, he smacked the door into the kitty litter box, spilling cinders across the ivory tiles. Taffy, awakened by the excitement, darted into action, slinking through his legs, sniffing her box and the spilled cinders, miffed at him for having uncovered her handiwork.

Using his hands, he swept the cinders into a pile.

"Forty dollars a month, Ms. Pussycat. How do you plan to repay?"

Taffy had already forgiven him and, traipsing through the pile, brushed across his leg, over and over, flipping her furry sides like a blade on a sharpening stone.

"I got it!" he said suddenly, his face full of a sinister but satisfied look.

Debbie snatched up her kitten in case he decided to rid her of her darling Taffy. Instead, crossing the room, he slid the kitty litter box into the fireplace, finding it a perfect fit.

# Crows and Sparrows

In divorce, the gods drop you from their lap, and the forces of the inevitable and adverse nudge you into the unknown, oblivious to your whimpers. Before you can protest or brace yourself, another source of harm and ruin shoves you into the body of the stranger beside you, so that you yourself become that stranger, first to the world, then to yourself. Alone, you wander into the forest of alienation where strangers introduce you to the age of self-help, Zen, and yogic self-centeredness. Although you strive to attain mental well-being, you, too angry for enlightenment, feel only discontented and rebellious. Or you seek spiritual elation in sex and food, but receive only disillusionment, the return of hunger and another day. You cannot suppress the scorn lacing your mind and will. You cannot unearth your good, kind self. Instead, shame and guilt hammer against the inside of your head. Or consternation vibrates through your ribs, tingling your fingertips.

In the aftermath of your marriage, you, pushed into a friendless world and roused to fear and pacing with uneasiness, cling to the structure of yourself. You hug a kind of mannequin of yourself, and in the creepy grayness of dreaded daybreaks, you lay fraught and sleepless over what is to come. Sweaty and weary, you sigh. The fight of your life is on.

* * *

First stop. My counselor. I am full of confession this morning. I tell her that every night, I dream I am driving a bulldozer around and around, making a perfect bowl in the earth. The hole grows and grows. BIack and deep, it looks like a crater on the moon. I run down into it, my feet sinking into the soft ground.

"And how do you feel about that?" Linda asks.

Next stop. The gym. It's good for me, releases my instinct as a builder. My mind and body unite in a drive for motion. Reason and impulse pull together. Below my conscious level is this concentration for action. Deep in my nature is this feeling for the physical. Over time, man has carpentered cities over valleys that he has excavated from stone. I am mind and body and will, the three of them in rhythm. I practically sing work songs on the calf machine.

Later, in the shower, compulsively rubbing my chest and shoulders and arms, I am an ape in my unconscious reflexes. Time will eventually remove all trace of me. But today, I am total.

Next. The bookstore where I work. Here I search among the customers for eternity's love in one encounter. I expect my soulmate to approach me with a discounted paperback. At times, this bookstore, with its high glass walls, seems to trap me like a fish in an aquarium, although, in shape, it fits into the city like another 55-gallon drum. What can I brave saying, during a twenty-second retail transaction, to grab the heart of my rescuer? The rest of the great, adventuresome world lies beyond me, through the spectacular pages of the National Geographic I shelve here. I am clerk #08.

We booksellers work commune-style: owning the store jointly but cultivating it individually. Gail manages her personal boundaries better than her staff. Frank warns me,

"Self. Self. Self. You're always thinking of yourself. Volunteer if you feel self-absorbed." He despises the egotistical side to me and accepts me only because of my kindly, good humor. Alice, dressed in black as supervisor of books on the benign supernatural, witches around her section at the top of the escalator, where all of humanity is her coven. In my desperate, overstimulated state, I wonder why I do not read anymore.

I have literary thoughts. Living here in Minneapolis reminds me of *The Fountainhead*. I imagine around the city the hero of this novel, Howard Roark. Or antihero, depending on one's moral evaluation of progress powered by the ego. I visualize him standing in the downtown doorways like a statue of Christ in a church alcove. I picture him gazing out of a large, dusty black pane in the Warehouse District, like a ghost from the fifties. I think of him standing, as a man outcast for his integrity, on distant bridges of the city above the black water of the mainstream. I see him sculpted into the pinnacles of the churches—Howard Roark, the highest in human development, poised on an I-beam above Minneapolis, solitary and defiant, or on any of the bony iron skeletons of buildings, the remote man working, wearing a green or white hardhat, staring over the city, seeing forever.

Roark and I and others like us scale the heights of heaven to ponder these regions of hell on earth. We are the climbers and the watchers, situating ourselves as lone spectators of our infernal world. We stand on the hood of this spaceship that is earth, facing the gusts of speed. We sit on rooftops, haul ourselves onto windy cliffs, and fly small planes through the clouds. We shinny up trees to reach widow's peaks, scrabble up goat trails to the mountaintops, and shoot up elevator shafts and into the clock towers of the city—to meditate above Pandemonium.

Then, as if overnight, she arrives in your life, a beautiful lover. There is life after divorce! You rejoice in your amazement that a lovely companion has saved you from solitude. You grow younger, and both of you rush toward the future, to redeem yourselves in the triumph of regained love. You bound into the days ahead of you, spirited and smiling, feeling great joy.

Her name is Beth. She is seven years older—and tough. All of my life, I have been drawn to tough, older women. I do not want to know why.

We discover that each of us married our friend—hers later became an alcoholic, mine a victim. But "The wounded can heal the wounded," according to her copy of The Kitchen Table Book of Wisdom.

She is a school teacher, and this is summer, her precious time off. But she is not sunning herself by her pool, reading back issues of School Arts to find creative ways to teach art to eight-year-olds. She works out several times a day—jogging in the morning, biking in the afternoon, and weightlifting in the evening. Her husband resented her fit physique. I worship it.

At this early stage, she calls us "fitness buddies." Every morning, she jogs three hard miles out into the hilly suburbs where she lives. Last month, she did a 500-mile bike ride through Wisconsin. Just this morning, she swam an easy mile at the Y, thirty laps in the Olympic-sized pool. All the while, I dangled my feet in the water, Aphrodite's young lover. I know that to be an Olympian's companion, I must run mountains with her, swim seas with her, and bike continents with her. The most significant conversation of our relationship will someday take place atop Pikes Peak. Most couples limit their love to sour codependency while vegetating in idling, traffic-locked cars, their bellies full of fast-food onion rings and chocolate shakes. Not Beth and me.

She owns a Chesapeake-blue condo in the burbs, a cute 3-year-old Honda, and earns fifty thousand a year as an art teacher for a Catholic private school where she has taught for the last eighteen years. I rent a dingy low-income efficiency downtown, ride the public bus, pretend to be a freelance writer, and accept money from my parents.

"Age. Just a set of numbers, right?" she says, sucking on her water bottle.

I do not respond. I am not thinking about our ages. I am thinking about our lifestyles. Around us, the room is still. Even the furniture looks petrified to hear what I am thinking.

I love her book The Kitchen Table Book of Wisdom. Romantic relationships begin and last, it tells me, when kept fun and friendly. Play exhilarates intimacy, it says. Play joins adults like kids. Play makes friends.

I am at her house. We are lying in bed. She has just told me that the Catholic priest at the private school where she teaches has been her lover for the last three years. I roll over and face her. "Then this chapter has already been written for me," I say. Also, a future-determining moment.

She gives her priest a name, Tom.

She gazes off into the darkness, as if expecting, or deserving, to be reproached. But I feel no righteous anger—she has not betrayed me or violated my confidence, but rather she has amazed me.

"A priest?" I say to myself, lying naked where, last evening, he, the priest, had lain naked.

I wonder if she changed the sheets.

I see a photograph of him, a big, bearded man in imperceptible, surreptitious guile as her "friend." Who'd suspect she is having sex with this priest?

So how is sex with this priest? That is all I can wonder, lying here, thinking of his cleric collar placed properly on her nightstand. I look down at my body, glad my stomach still appears flat. Beth still sits on the edge of her bed, waiting for me to react in rage.

"So you love him?"

"I'm in the process of breaking it off with him," she says back.

* * *

You cannot remember when—how long ago and at which instant—you broke with yourself, with your bond of faith and honesty. When you hear planes whisking through the blue, see bright taxis carrying excited families into the shopping district, and smell tasty dinners in the hallway of your apartment building, with chatter and laughter beyond the walls, you realize, as your heart withers and hardens into a plum pit, you are alone.

Two evenings later, as I lie in her bed, naked once again, she arrives with a new revelation about our future together, one that hints at the ugliness to come.

"I feel guilty about this," she says.

I roll over to face Beth. I already know she is about to kick my heart out like the bottom of a rusted bucket.

"I still love him."

"I think I should leave."

I am furious, or think I am, and rise to dress.

"Wait…please."

Hers is a lazy, half-hearted plea to keep me, and only for this gross mockery of me do I despise her. As she attempts to stop me from leaving her condo, stepping in front of me and grabbing my hand as I reach for a doorknob, I feel we are in a prime-time romantic drama written by Danielle Steele.

Then, the horror, the unimaginable, starts. I cannot hear her apologies over the pounding of my resentment. Soon, both of us feel unseemly together, tarnished by arguments. Petulant, quarrelsome, and discouraged by our sudden incompatibility, we both agree to break it off.

What dismays me, in the days after we parted, is how brief, how fleeting, the relationship turned out to be. But I am not to blame. Rather, I simply retaliated for her bad conduct. I am blameless, I decide.

I go to see Mary, an older, writer friend. "I am an incubus," I tell her. I drain women.

"A what?" She squints into the sun blazing across the outdoor café, and from the age on her face, I see for sure that she's too old to become my next victim.

Is anyone well-read today? I scoot my chair closer and whisper my incredible secret to her. My friend Crystal can confirm this demon in me, I add.

Mary gives me the eye.

"Is—was—Crystal," she asks, "drained?"

No, Crystal was an elusive quarry.

Mary relaxes. "Because my friend has a daughter named Crystal—that's why I ask."

I mock a face of disgust.

"No, but I think that's fascinating, really," she continues.

She is my Zen master of sorts. I need her advice. I tell her I lose the friendships of these "drained" women.

"Well, as a writer, you court rejection," she says, "so maybe these conquests...maybe they offset all that."

I think about this.

"Maybe you're a satyr," she says.

I smile. She proves to be literary after all. I pull out my notepad to jot down the word: satyr.

* * *

Bursting into the streets to search for your savior, you become aware of the hopeless size of the world around you. Seeking companionship, you might walk for the next thirty years. At the start, you pass only zombies of despair huddled at bus stops, littered and grimy. Divorce, you note, dropped you into the low-income district. Old scrub women with massive baggy arms do not see the handsome youth in you anymore, and young office women modeling smart outfits detect the trouble, the desperation, in your stride. All the world, it seems, senses your uneasiness. Even bums eye you, wary of your soul. Or you feel invisible, when not ugly. Buses blow soot at you—you are too sensitive, you admonish yourself. Too self-critical, you add.

Downtown, attractive, moneyed couples snicker at you. Uptown, predaceous gays smile at your vulnerable self-consciousness—you are curious how men comfort one another. Day after day, fear and hope kick and slap and shake each other in a tussle for your soul. When you feel at your worst, crows fly low to cackle over you, "...John Lonely, John Lonely, pessimism is you, John Lonely, John Lonely..."

Tonight, the good and evil in me are in a dead heat. I balance myself on my bike on the 1st Avenue Bridge, gazing through the smelly mist at the lighted towers of the city. The mighty river bridge trembles as cars race past me—everyone is hurrying to be not where they are. Weightless on the suspended vaults of concrete spanning the river, minute under the skyline of geometric mountains of glass and steel, I feel painfully little and alone.

I phone my Linda.

"Linda, why is everyone so afraid to laugh and love today?"

"People are afraid of being hurt."

"Aren't they more afraid of not living?"

"John," she addresses me officially, "are you interested in resuming our sessions?"

"All of my life I have yearned to be someone's hero."

"And you have been," she reminds me. "Several times." She pauses. "How's the new job going?" She is beginning to assess.

Having her on the phone, I grow desperate for her understanding. "We're all dying, Linda, dying in spirit."

Now, I sound gravely troubled.

"I hear you're hurting—"

"I'm not hurting," I quickly correct her. "I'm perplexed."

I worry whether I see the modern world clearly. I perceive an edgy land of incertitude, in which people remain unfamiliar, talk is generic, and feelings go unidentified. Life, as it seems, has neither limits nor possibilities. People are as vague as dreams. They seem as constrained by caution and reluctance as the low-rise apartment buildings and office parks that interlock over the land.

"I hear you, John. But I think in your case," she says, "you spend so much time being charming that you come off as if not having a care in the world. Now, you've called me at my home. Come in Monday morning. Bring a payment."

Love drowns like a sweet, pale girl too dazed to swim, her mouth bubbling out life, her nightgown flowing upward beautifully in the cold black water.

* * *

"What do you want?" my friend Phillip puts to me from Philadelphia.

What I want, I answer him carefully, is a good, complete friend and lover. I keep a picture of her in my head, in a vignette, framed by maturity and wisdom. Is my request of life reasonable? Or do I take what comes along? Modern life entails this kind of oxymoronic free-for-all for possessions, this materialistic brawl softened and disguised by laws and ethics.

"Good women do not root through"—I am flustered in my search for a wise, clarifying remark—"through the Dumpster of Souls."

"Dumpster of Souls..." Phillip repeats, almost singing the phrase. Then he tells me to step into the body of another man.

Okay, I could dress like Bruce Springsteen. I could impersonate Fabio. I could portray Romeo. I could double for Nicolas Cage. I could pretend to be F. Scott Fitzgerald or imitate Jackson Brown. I could pose as Van Gogh. Or I could be John.

I have plenty of advice, but no help.

"Breathe well," Craig, from his holy orb in my conscience, reminds me.

"Respect the dignity of each individual," Amanda, behind a tree in the park, whispers.

"Be true to yourself," Gary, from voicemail, contributes.

In Beth's house reads a plaque: "Live well, laugh often, love much."

But in the end, all I can do is to think furiously to form my mental picture of myself.

Sunday afternoons press against my chest, as if my soul were in the vice of the week's end and another's beginning. I feel short and slow and heavy, like a settling house. Depression floats over the hemisphere of my brain like heavy gray clouds. I pray to reach Monday, to rejoin society in routine. I pray to belong again. I pray.

Monday morning. Time to see Linda. In her office, I am heavy-hearted and fixated on the past. My deceit of myself, I say, has cost me my place in the world, in Rhode Island, where I have lived for seven years, waiting tables.

I talk about Craig. He is my editor at Utne Reader. Well, not really my editor. More like he takes pity on me, as well as takes my calls during which I whine for an assignment, and he gives me none, smelling instability on my end. Instead, he meets me for coffee, every third Friday, when he needs to feel benevolent.

"Sponge people up," he smiles. "Don't bat them away—and don't forget to breathe."

Whenever I meet with Craig, I note his remarkable mellowness, first as a busy, important editor and second as a father, husband and 46-year-old. I assume that Craig, an adherent of Utne thoughtfulness, has gone peacefully hippie over the years. Or by chanting as a Zen Buddhist, he has purified himself. Anyway, I have noticed that he does breathe slowly, calmly.

In the coffee shop below his office, where he can keep me at arm's length, he sits breathing like the sea. So self-controlled is Craig that he seems to balance, on his head, a stack of a thousand bricks. Living, for him, is restful. In discussions, his mind hums like small, tight wheels on a sporty coupe. I can learn from him.

But he is not my friend, I tell Linda. My true friends are gone. Ted is in Hampton, Virginia. Walt went to Prague to be the editor of a revolutionary newspaper. When Walt called me last week, he sounded different, himself screwy, full of abstract chatter about spirituality. His Prague paper folded, so now he runs a yoga school. Also, he is in love. I don't recognize him, nor he me.

I ask Linda about the changes people undergo.

"Well, your friend Walt's been halfway around the world," she replies, "and you—you've been to hell and back."

I shift, feeling wearied by it all.

"But you are getting better," she says.

Take the next bus, she adds. Love and safety will wait. Weirdness is not my friend, she remarks, and there is no punk called fear. Inhale, exhale. See the beauty. Have friends. Be a Spartan sharing the distance. Be in the universe. There is no incubus, only crows and sparrows, no life by cellophane, no lone spectators, only the audience around us.

I tell her I forgot to bring a payment.

Back at the bookstore, I find myself encountering a customer.

"So, are you taking a trip to Bermuda?" I ask a pretty woman needing a travel book about the islands. What thrills me about being a bookseller is cozying up to strangers. She and I are walking together as I show her the travel section. A friendly, outdoorsy gal with a bouncy stride, she is naturally shining her smile on me.

"Yeah, in February, with friends. It'll be cool."

"Oh, sounds nice. Friends from work?"

My smile is equally jaunty and also a tad frolicsome, to the extent that my small, innocent questions play around me like puppies.

"No, from church."

"Church?" I stop. "It's nice to hear that, if I may say so."

Joy, like a puppy, jumps into her arms and licks her face.

"Oh, I know," she gushes. "It's been the best thing in my life. Religion has delivered me from the great modern mix-up."

I like her. Jackie, her name is. She is, as they say, okay.

"I can't wait," she goes on. "A whole week in Bermuda."

"So," I resume, "what'd you plan to do there, for a whole week?"

In my secret hope of someday outrunning the ugly ostrich of loneliness, I am inviting myself along with her.

Jackie and I are on the stairs taking us to the ground floor when she tells me that she's really going to Bermuda because, there, her boyfriend can receive experimental chemotherapy, their final resort against his leukemia.

"Oh, it's okay," she assures me. "We've been dealing with this for a long time."

Okay? Death is a giant chasing her boyfriend down the beanstalk. Not okay.

"Are you all right?" she asks me, smiling.

I say yes, but I am not all right. I manage to find her a book and to make sure it's the one she wants. But I'm glad when she leaves. I go upstairs and sit in the lounge. I don't care who sees me.

I am not a loner—but I am lonely. I am not as courageous as I should be, in a lonesome world. Many walk alone, I notice. Many men, many women. Actually, I do not want companionship. What I want is courage.

As I sit here talking with Linda, sunken in the lounge chair, I realize that to feel and seem normal is to settle slightly. Life after divorce is a hard-boiled afterlife, a tough existence after innocence and good conscience, a later period in one's life when hope is stained. Divorce seems both a brand on the shoulder and a wrinkle on the cheek, a mark both of discredit and age.

At thirty-four, I boat miles upriver to a great waterfall. At forty-four, I arrive at the headwaters. At fifty-four, I reach the low sandbars, rocky shores, and heavy water shouldering in a pool against the earth dam. At sixty-four, I hear the hiss of the dragon living in the waterfall and smell its zesty, organic watery breath. At seventy-four, mist drenches me at the edge where the dragon awaits. At eighty-four, I will drop to the center of the earth, and the vacation of my life will end.

But this is still only Tuesday, and I have my cat to feed.

# Alone

For the first time in two years, Stephen did not phone his wife from work all day, and that evening, as he waited for her bus at the station, patted on the face by a snappy breeze, the day he had endured without talking to her convinced him he may never see her again.

He had been calling her for the last three hours, but her cell phone went straight to voicemail every time. It was no secret they hadn't been getting along lately. Just last week, their neighbor down the hall frowned and eyed them warily after they'd had another big argument. Their fights were stupid, too. Her meddlesome parents. His standoffish attitude. Their credit cards. Life!

This morning, they separated without a word to each other, and this afternoon, she didn't tell him when she'd arrive at the bus station. Now, her phone was turned off, the sky was dark, the hour becoming late. As he paced the length of the station pavilion, from the dimly lit bathroom doors to the last section of concrete, she was vastly left out, lost from him, stranded at the distant, long-ago departure of this morning.

He could only guess when she'd arrive. He tried to figure out which road the bus would take into town, but the new highway brought traffic in on a criss-cross grid of roads and streets. Over and over, he whirled on the soft ends of his shoes and gaped into a windy blackness varnished by a dry mist of parking lot light. The station operator told him fourteen commuter buses came in nightly, sometimes fewer, sometimes more. Every ten minutes or so, a sooty bus arrived at the station and idled in a junction around the depot. Some roared in on the dark service road behind the parking lot. Others lumbered along the lighted avenue and eased to a stop, mooring like a cargo ship.

For Stephen, the hour was late, 11:12 by his phone. Time again, he checked his cell and called hers. No texts, no voicemail. Nothing. Maybe the battery died in her phone. Maybe the charger cord wasn't working. Maybe she'd broken her phone. He could call their neighbor and ask if she had been home. Better yet, he could call her girlfriend. But she'd immediately suspect him of having murdered her, and now he was putting in an advance performance of innocence. He could always call her sister, but his brother-in-law had friends on the Kerrymont police force, and they'd throw a dragnet over his neighborhood after putting him in hand-cuffs. If he called her mother, the governor would soon be involved.

So he called his home only to hear his own pathetic voice on the answering machine. He kicked his toe against the walk, an uncivil quirk of his that annoyed Anne.

Over the last hour and a half, Stephen had observed all fourteen buses come in, each time with hope and disap-pointment. He counted and recounted all fourteen, now uniformly parked and in bed for the night. Except for a glossy, candy-apple-red tour bus, each bus had squeezed onto the side street accessing the station and, with a final black belch, rolled into the rounding lanes, screeching into a space for the night. Taxis, glowing with smoky-yellow interior lights, had all left the deserted station. The station had closed, too. There was nothing inside except the continuous silhouette of rounded terminal chairs and the red and green eyes of computers left running overnight. With the wind picking up, leaves started scampering and rattling across the walk toward him, as if rushing to sympathize with him. A metal hook, dangling from the end of a rope, clanged against a flagpole.

Then, in a leap of his heart, he spotted one approaching. Its large lit interior supplied a ceremonial touch to its arrival. He jogged to the edge of the pavement as it emerged from the black night and revved alongside the pavilion to begin its wide turn into the lot. He hoped to see her in one of the windows. At first, the cloudy insides of the bus looked empty, but then he noticed a gray blur sitting at the rear.

Anne!

As the belching bus rolled past him, he grinned, the excitement quickening his pulse. She would get off the bus in mere minutes! He yanked up his drooping pants, patted the sides of his curly hair, and moved closer to the bus as it came to a stop. He felt foolish for even thinking she wouldn't be back. He wanted to tell her he loved her and that he never wanted to be apart from her again. Feverishly, he wanted to hold her hand and express that they needed to make changes in their lives together and that he was willing to put in the effort.

But when the bus door opened and the lights brightened, the shape that he thought was Anne's produced before his eyes an older woman with a hard-looking face. The woman didn't even look at him as he backed up to let her off the bus. He watched her awkward body clamber down the steps, winter boots knocking, and she walked past him as if he didn't matter.

He started up the steps of the bus, to scan around inside for Anne, but the driver quickly informed him there was no one else onboard. As he stepped back off, his mind went crazy for worry. Blurry, chaotic images of a police station, a hospital, of official-looking people telling him of an accident, all flashed before his eyes. He saw Anne's parents in Connecticut. He saw his own mother in Kentucky.

Sweat leaked into the crevices of his hands. A cold, coastal wind burned tears in his eyes. Where was she?

The ring of his cell phone in his jacket jolted him. A sick feeling lodged in the pit of his stomach. He stood terrified. Were the police calling? The ER?

He pulled his phone out and answered the call.

"Hello?" he said in a hollow low tone, feeling he was speaking into a dark tunnel leading to light.

"Hi, hon."

Anne! He was stunned, too surprised to speak.

"Stephen?"

"Hi!" he burst out, pressing the phone to his cheek.

"Wow, somebody's glad to hear from me. I'm on the bus. We just passed Steerforth Hill, so I should be at the depot, oh, in twenty minutes."

Fourteen buses, sometimes more, the operator had said.

"I'm already here waiting for you."

She paused.

"You're at the station now?"

Stephen grinned in the night air.

"Yes."

"But...how'd you know what time I was coming?"

"I didn't."

"You mean, you've been waiting all this time?"

"Of course. For you."

"Oh, God. Stephen, I'm so sorry."

He could feel the embers of a hundred fires, a hundred spats, instantly extinguish and vanish into the night. He stepped back under the pavilion, away from the wind, to wait for her bus, staying on the phone with her the whole time.

# The Houseplant Generation

Although they had agreed when to have a child—two to three years from his next birthday—she, dissatisfied with the vague distance of this date and troubled with his reasoning, would spring the issue on him, he thought, with calculating spite harmful to their new and uncomplicated marriage.

"There's really no ideal time to have a child," she would ultimately say.

That she confronted him when the air between them seemed freest of worry only made him uncooperative, defensive, equally antagonistic, and resentful of her tactics.

"We've discussed this a hundred times, honey," Mike said.

They had.

"Why do you keep, I don't know, blaming me?"

His reasoning came from the yuppie spirit of his generation—to own a starter condo and to earn high numbers before having children. His bachelor's degree in graphic arts had secured him an illustrator job that paid well—earning more meant management, which had no openings at present. Her mother, by contrast, while still a teenager and married to a factory worker overseas in the Navy, carried Lisa to full-term by herself. So neither agreed on the conditions, the environment, of parenting.

This afternoon, on a crowded road heading to the shopping mall but boxed into the wrong lane, behind cars turning into a 7-11, they again sweltered from the unresolvable showdown of this issue. He was yelling at drivers around him, and she was glaring ahead, both, in a moment, not lovers but enemies. What startled him was her easily incensed defense, how quickly she cried out in oppression, supposedly, to his fear of becoming a father. Here on the road, she was unbearable. The sagging power lines and smutty cinderblock apartment buildings made her look ugly. He could not possibly stay with her. Never would bring Jonathon into this neighborhood, either. In truth, he'd never be ready for a child.

They had named the baby already, Jonathon Corbett if a boy, Claire Ellen if a girl. He found himself hoping for a son—"Let's have him in July, a Cancer just like us." He worried whenever she mentioned him by name too frequently, as if little Jonathon were his nephew coming next week to stay the summer.

From the parking lot to the long stacks of shopping carts, he ambled behind her, sulking. But when she turned to him between the automatic doors, he looked tickled with the smooth and quiet ride of the shopping cart, with its lubricated wheels and rattleless frame, responsive to turns as he playfully serpentined like a little boy.

"Jonathon will ride in there in a few years," she offered as a truce, making a goofy face at him. She waited for him to grin before she looked where she was walking—into a display of houseplants.

Seeing him surrender to smiles made the half-off discount sign in front of her more a reward than a chance.

"Let's get one," she suggested, stooping, already examining the yellow arrow-shaped tags tied loosely onto the highest stems across this leafy stretch of floor. The plants, in a jumble of different greens, celebrated the first week of spring with the frivolous decor of retail. Last week, a salad bar had stood here.

"The apartment could really use one," she said.

Leaning over the cart, he watched her step into the display, reading tags, "Needs 'high light'…needs 'low light' and water." He helped her narrow the selection. Not liking the color of the acacias, she let him choose a bushy but lopsided plant, with camouflage-pattern leaves.

After he had tiptoed and sidled through the community of plants, navigating around branches and pots toward his favorite, he noticed her watching him with an expression oddly benevolent and affectionate, in the aftertaste of their argument—as if by selecting the plant, he had just given her a gift. He noticed, too, several shoppers eyeing his plant, as if imagining it in their homes. When he stood clutching the black rubber pot, with the leaves hissing as they brushed his shoulder and cheek and reached over the aisle, an unlikely sense of pride and ownership exuded from him, and for a moment the entire store seemed to applaud.

Wheeling the cart, loaded with the spreading plant, felt good, too. Transporting this subtropical shrub, this life aboard, gave him custody of a new responsibility. He rolled the cart slowly, both hands on the clear red handle. He walked obediently behind his wife, stopping patiently whenever she reached into the shelves, following dutifully as she moved to the next section. They had not spoken since selecting the plant, and the silence seemed mutually peaceful. Moving in a loosely spaced and wavering line, they acted older, like parents.

With his lips rested lightly together, he looked content and composed, protective in his new position of driving the cart. All the while, the branches rose loftily in front of him, attracting glances and smiles. A stately lady in a business suit peered into his cart as she passed, her powdered angular face inquiring of the usefulness, the reward, of his plant. Others noticed him, his self-pleased smile. When they reached the checkout counter, the cashier, letting him keep the plant in the cart, commented, in a coquettish insinuation of her own dissolved family, "Looks like somebody's moving in."

Blushing, overpowered by the coarse smile of the cashier, he looked to his wife for help. She was shuffling credit cards. The flanking checkout lines riddled him with stares as if waiting for his reply. After all, something or someone was moving in.

Leaving the store brought more stares. Free of the close and watchful aisles, he strode proudly with the cart, ready to take his plant home.

"What do you think of it?" he asked her, crossing the lot, aware of a man in a car watching them.

She answered him by taking his arm.

Driving home, smoothly changing lanes to prevent tipping the plant, he glanced frequently at his wife and at the spotted leaves that dangled between the seats and divinely dressed her profile. As soon as the leaves stayed still, they sprang loose from between the seats again, causing him to grin wryly at her.

"It's going to be a big plant," she remarked, more to see him look over at her than to hear him agree.

With the car parked on their street, he unloaded the plant, saying, "Here we go," as he gripped the soft rubber pot and lifted. She gathered and aimed the branches through the wedge of space left by the retracted front seat.

"Careful, honey," he warned.

Then she held open the door to the apartment house. Careful not to touch the walls or the banister, he moved quickly, nimbly, up the flight, stepping faster and lighter with the plant than ever without it. He stood waiting for his wife at the apartment door before she reached the first landing.

Inside, he set the plant in the corner, turned the base so that the branches looked balanced with the converging walls, raised the Venetian blinds, and stepped back, hands on his hips. Hurrying to share in arranging the plant, she dropped the shopping bags beside the refrigerator and, moving silently over the carpet, followed him into the living room, vigilant of his handling of the plant.

"What about in this corner?" she suggested.

"No, it'll get more light here. Remember, 'high light.'"

They both stared at the plant, absorbing the scene, the upturned, translucent leaves, luminously green, looking electric.

"Should we give it water?" he asked, trying to include her in the task.

She moved quickly to the plant, felt the dirt, and said while still stooped, "No, not for a while. It feels recently watered."

When she stayed on her knees, he noticed her watching him, her small lips pressed into a sly expression.

"What?"

She said nothing, just wore a soft smile.

Then she stood, saying, "Do you think it'll last two to three years from your next birthday?"

His grin satisfied her, and the nuance of her remark stayed intact, ringing lightly through both of them. He stood thinking of Jonathon until she returned and slid a clear glass dinner plate beneath the pot, to catch the water.

"So, tell me, what do you think of it?" he asked, wanting more than a typical remark.

"It's nice to bring a little life into a house," she answered, arranging the branches.

# Shadow Box

From inside the house, the feature resembles a kind of alcove recessed into space, a three-sided miniature room overhanging the street. From the outside, the shadow box window, huge but inconspicuous, replicates the dimensions of the Greek-columned porch on which it stands. To the new couple moving into the apartment beside it, the milky rain of light in the window possesses an undiscovered purpose, a place to explore.

Michael, in particular, is spellbound. A month ago, during the realtor's tour, the projected niche immediately enchanted him. Its ethereal and serene glow drew him away from the group, including his wife, the realtor, and the house lady. When he first stepped into its standing space, he felt an intense energy surround him, a presence, an occupation of another living force.

More every day, the reduced proportions of the space charmed him, especially the short pieces of white baseboard, snipped and tucked to fit and frame a square of carpet the size of a card table. He adored the bands of rough weatherboards, in foot-long pieces around the three windows. They rise to a flat-paneled ceiling soaked in the glow of recent antique-white enamel.

"What a cute little room," his wife declared later on the evening of the tour. She cherished the trilateral sets of Venetian blinds illuming the umber carpet inside the window with radially hatched lines of lemon sunlight. Was the shrine-shaped feature more ornamental than functional, more indulgent and playful than practical or planned?

Over the last month, Michael has returned to the protruding space every evening, finding spokes of moonlight radiating inside. Again, in this little room, he feels the same tumid pressure, the kind in a cold car. He likens the space to the confessional in the unlocked Romanesque church on his childhood street. He'd sit in the confessional, letting the immediate darkness soothe him, itself absolve him.

Tonight, through the blinds on the right side of the window, he sees outside into the dark, then inside their apartment where his wife stands. As he watches her, he feels in his suspended, outward angle a detached mood, a feeling of isolation from seeing his wife without him and within another compartment of the house, this fascinating shadow box. In his insular booth above the earth, he suddenly becomes aware of himself as a frail and single person.

By now, they've mastered with their wrists and fingers the rhythmic technique to unsticking the door lock. They've discovered how to glide silently along the dim hallways of the house, under a thunderous white-trim archway, and up a spiraling oak banister, avoiding noisy treads and loose floorboards. They've now territorialized every dimension of their apartment, scenting the bathroom and kitchen with numerous melting soaps, filling the windowsills with potted plants, and dressing the fireplace mantel with potpourri baskets, soap tins, and colored stones found during walks along the inlet.

Neither the landlady downstairs nor the tenant across the hall has shown any interest in the miniature room. So the unclaimed appeal of the alcove is all theirs.

"Honey, what do you think of the little room," he asks, with the newness of the historic Greek Revival house settled comfortably.

Ellen's been propping up postcards of Maxfield Parrish paintings along the mantelpiece. His question interrupts her, and when she turns, she knocks a few postcards off the ledge. She stoops and gathers them in her hands.

"There's a ghost living in there," she announces, standing.

The word ghost strikes him not as a literal embodiment, but as a verification of the tingling sensation he has experienced whenever standing in the space, together with the illusion of hovering over the street, in this place as isolated as a scenic overlook.

He sits up on the sofa. Her claim suggests a kind of paranormal invasion, a supernatural trespassing.

"Really, ghosts?"

"No, just one," she corrected.

He has known her to make this kind of absurd remark. Once, she claimed that, in a former life, she had been Lord Byron's lover. Another time, she insisted she had seen her exact portrait in the National Gallery of Art, somewhere amid a series of retrospectives of Flemish Renaissance painters. Her painted face gazed serenely at her. Of late, Ellen has decided she will reincarnate as a butterscotch cat.

"It's probably the person who owned the house," she says of the presence in the shadow box.

From day to day, he observes the way she, when either leaving or entering the apartment, swivels her head ever so evenly, like an owl, with her large black-almond eyes protruding toward the shadow box. She stares down the hallway and into the miniature room, seeing something. Her catatonic, bewitched gaze startles him.

"What!" he snaps.

His wife is entranced by the shadow box.

"Honey, what is it?" he demands, stepping into her view.

"Thought I saw something."

"What?" he presses, not willing to let her dismiss it. "A person?"

"I just don't know."

He believes her. She has detected a specter in the dusty bars of sunlight filtering through the slanted sets of blinds.

"Show me what's in there," he braved asking.

She again glances down the hall, into the phosphorus bars of moonlight criss-crossing in this little glass room.

"Oh, Michael, there's something in there right now!"

He starts toward the shadow box. When he turns to see if she has followed, his jaws clinch, insisting she follow.

"Show me," he says.

Without him, she steps inside, cleanly and calmly, and glances out the windows. Shadows of leaves cast by a street light flicker upon her skin. Abandoned, Michael quickly follows her and recognizes at once the sensation, not disconcerting, but close and unified. Briefly, they stand as figurines inside a glass display. They press together, shoulder touching shoulder. He clenches her hand, interlocking a few fingers.

"It's just us," he hears her say.

# The Last Sailor

Like a heavy antique placed in a show of pride beside a laughably light reproduction, he challenges the authenticity of this commercialized seaside town. Wrapped in a wool overcoat even during summer, he ambles up and down the slate walk alongside his sagging bungalow, around which the historical society has orchestrated the refacing of shop fronts, a nip and tuck of overloaded Victorian eaves, and a stiff upward stretch of tin roofs and chimneys, along with a kind of architectural liposuction of the bulging structural backs and bellies.

He watches, his hair yellowed by a lifelong tour at sea. He knows what happens to small towns that dandy up and shrink-wrap their real estate. Here on snooty Historic Hill, higher telephone poles accommodate new taut wires. Bring on the electronic wizardry and Wi-Fi jazz of this new century, disguised with old-town appeal. Bedeck these timber log Colonials with a tidy business office, computer inside a varnished roll-top desk.

The sailor and his small house of few rooms, paned with wavy glass, directly face our apartment. To the left of us, a yarn shop, and to the right, Dumpsters. Lots of them. To the east of the sailor's reading window, the golden steeple soars over the St. Mark's Georgian church, a tourist landmark, spotlighted in the misty coastal night, ornate and majestic in the blue of day, solemn and lordly in the dismal winter. The adorable burying ground, rendered adorable by the town's historical society, fits neatly between the sailor's rightmost window and the white clapboards of the church hall. If the sailor were to press his face against a window, he'd never see the sea.

From the start, he captivates us with his ancient appearance, his bona fide wool attire of a dumpy black fedora and threadbare reefer, a blackness draping him like that which hangs from a creepy undertaker. Jill often remarks that he looks as if he just stepped out of another century. Our town is supposedly out of another century, gaslit and cobblestone, with showy, pinnacled belfries and spires, all in suburbanized history. We have daily walking tours of the Nashberg House, which bears the most panoramic widow's peak in town, with dizzying views of the vibrant windjammers moored in the inlet.

The sailor's Irish, we figure, likely a native of Ireland. Through his window in the daytime, we see a lace doily overhanging a bureau, topped with a delicate assembly of small sepia portraits set in black-iron oval frames, along with various Virgin Mary figurines and a centrally placed rosary—all the customary Irish Catholic memorabilia of ancestral homage.

Jill and I, in our enchantment of him, turn into peeping Toms. Walking late, we search the churchyard where we often spot him, standing alone in the shadows, within a time-bound silhouette. After trailing him along a graceful slate walkway curving around the above-ground crypts, we find his silhouette in the light of his window. The shade's drawn. Seated and still, he appears to be reading. The cracked, waxy-brown shade hits us with an undeniable feeling of antiquity.

"You think he gets lonely?" Jill whispers, in a long remote gaze upon his lambent window blind glowing like an electric pumpkin.

I don't answer; I'm mesmerized by the tawny, oily radiance of the shade, like lacquered pews nearest the altar.

"Yes," I finally say.

Later in bed, Jill wonders whether he's safe by himself. Does a daughter check on him? What happened to his wife? I'm wondering how he can tolerate the beered-up tourists from New Jersey.

In the morning, I slow as I pass his window—there he is! The blind is up, and he's seated close to the window, reading a hefty book. The large pane of glass before him intensifies him, presents him as larger than life. At the same time, the sun blanches him, and from his crystalline channels of skin, the pink flesh of tender youth returns.

What is he reading? The Bible? *Moby-Dick*? He doesn't look up, so I keep walking.

At home, Jill soon projects a similarity between her father and the sailor. That I don't see. When she compares him to my father, I'm utterly at a loss. I've heard what the sea air can do to a woman.

"Is he up?" Jill asks as I peer at his house from our darkened window.

We are obsessed with him.

* * *

For the next two months, Jill and I, ourselves overimpressed by the colonial charm of this town, partake in a trendy spring celebration of maritime history called Narragansett Days. On Easter, those of us who live in the refurbished colonial houses on Historic Hill, us retro yuppies, place delightful electric candles in our windows. Speakers play Irish folk music. Trinity Street, the first street in town, dating back to 1690, plugs into the twenty-first century.

Then, through May, Jill and I mingle with crowds at our neighborhood block parties. Later in the month, we join the coastal fad of owning an affable black Labrador ringed with a dashing red collar. We name this one Jasper for no good reason.

In June, Jill, looking up from her section of the evening paper, remarks that we have not seen the sailor since winter.

"Not once?" I looked up the computer. "Really? It's been that long?"

We forgot him, and we didn't miss him. Days and days wheeled past, and we hadn't thought of him once.

We sit quietly, astonished by our sudden discovery of his absence from our minds. The next day, Jill buys an over-sized lovable Paddington Bear—a loudly dressed sailor bear. He wears a canary-yellow rain hat, magazine-red rubber galoshes, and a forceful blue stadium coat with tiny wooden pegs used as buttons.

"I saw our sailor today!" Jill cries out, bustling into our apartment a few days later. "He was at the Seaport Spa, honey. He's a long-time member." She lets my face fall in disbelief. "That's right. He's down there now if you wanna see him…playing basketball with a bunch of kids."

Seaport Spa? Playing basketball? My head reels.

The haughty Seaport Spa stands well at a distance from the neon-lit eateries for locals. Around the Lifestyle-Center, as the spa is also called, are boutique hotels, and around them are cruising yachts, which bespeak of New York money.

"No way!"—I erupt in astonishment—"You're kidding?"

"Honey, get this"—she rushes up to me—"he works at the sanitation department, on health leave right now."

My one clear thought is that I must look maniacal.

"He's not as old as you think," she tells me.

She makes me ask.

"Well, how old is he?"

I sound sore.

"Probably, hmm, barely fifty. Anyway, he said hello to me." In her smug satisfaction, she adds, "And the young kids really seem to take to him."

The Seaport Spa! Playing basketball? Sanitation department? The old dude betrayed me. He slipped out of character. He had sold his antique essence for a reproduction.

That evening, hunting for him through our bedroom window, I spot him shuffling down the block in an overcoat toward where, beyond the remodeled seafaring history, the town turns into pulsating discos, all-night liquor stores, and the rowdy swinger crowd. Jill joins me at the window where together we watch him, confused, disenchanted, and disappointed. In an instant, he's like any other person.

Around us, Jill and I have lots of lovely furniture—a Victorian fainting couch, cane chairs, ball-and-claw foot tables, a Ben Franklin clock, and a double-door chifforobe faced with intricate leaf carvings. All reproductions, all filled with pine pulp, all laminated with superior hardwood. All of our furniture, in fact, however lavish in gleam, are chain-store reproductions. They don't impress anyone.

As with the sailor, once they lose their intrinsic value, they become easy to overlook.

# The Scratchboard Project

"Draw Shanice?" Mrs. Sharpe said through the screen door, wiping her hands on a towel. She glanced down at the sketchpad under my arm. Behind her, shirtless little Black kids were hopping around. They opened the screen door themselves and flooded around me on the porch.

"Everyone, this is Josh."

They looked up, and in that instant, as I looked down at all of them, I saw for the first time the world in X-ray–black-and-white shapes floating before my eyes like objects tied to a mobile, just as my art teacher, Mr. Thompson, wanted us to see for the scratchboard project.

The scratchboard project: an exercise in negative and positive relationships. You started with a piece of board with black coating on it, and you had to take your etcher and etch out a drawing, make a white image out of solid blackness. Essentially, you had to draw in reverse. You left what you ordinarily drew in and took away what you ordinarily left white.

The rules for the project were simple:

1.    Choose someone in school you don't know.
2.    Go to their house and study them "gesturally."
3.    Reverse them, through a series of sketches later to be used as templates for transfers to the scratchboard.

Naturally, I had procrastinated, and now every kid I knew from every decent house in town had been taken. I ended up here, in the next town, Bolivar, on this god-forsaken porch. Shanice Sharpe was the meanest Black militant bitch in school. Her little brothers stood gazing up at me with placid faces that I was sure would turn inside out and hiss like demons.

Mrs. Sharpe shooed them away from my legs.

"Josh is in Shani's grade in school," she said. "He lives over in Harpers Ferry."

"Alabama?" said the littlest one.

She led me inside to a small, dark room crowded with junk I couldn't see well. Chairs, boxes, and bags of aluminum cans—all were in our way, along with stacks of Washington Post TV guides. There were Sony TV boxes used as furniture, holding up gigantic boxes of Cheerios and Pampers. On the walls were so many pictures of Black children with shining white teeth that I couldn't see what was underneath—wood, mud, straw, or aluminum siding with bullet holes. There were crucifixes, too; not the good Irish-Catholic kind, but cheap-looking white plastic ones from a five-and-ten somewhere.

All the kids were yapping at once. Shanice's brother Tyrone came out of nowhere. He was so enormous he had to lower his head under the doorway. He had on sneakers that were as big as snowshoes, an orange tank top that came down to his knees like a dress, and a cap turned backward. The sight of me standing in his house took him by surprise, and he stood there shyly.

"Tyrone, you wanna show Josh your trophy?" she said, speaking to us like a kindergarten teacher. "Go on now."

I followed him into an even smaller room. Nintendo games on the floor, posters of Shaq and Black girls in bikinis all over the place.

"Here," he said, his big arm swinging around.

All I saw were greasy Black fingers around a shiny silver trophy that looked stolen. I had to say something.

"You won that?"

He turned around and stood up against me. I barely came up to the zero on his jersey.

"Yeah, I won that. What'd you think? Came in a box of Cheerios?"

Truthfully, yeah. He might have had me alone, but I wasn't as scared of him as he thought, even if he was three times bigger.

"Where you live in Harpers Ferry, little man? Ridge Street?"

"Polk Street," I said.

"Pork who?" He broke into a stupid snicker, his shiny Black face all scrunched up. "Shit, Jed Clampett Jr."

Then he asked me something in Black lingo, but I didn't understand and stood staring back at him.

"Damn, dude," he said, coming in clear now and flipping his big hands around like a LL Cool J or something, "you want a Coke or not?"

Mrs. Sharpe, appearing at the door, looked concerned for the situation.

"Tyrone," she said, "remember what we talked about?"

He went into his big shy kid routine, plopping his huge body down on a spring bed, squeaking it to death.

"Yes, ma'am, my manners."

He was so shame-faced and meek, beaten down by his mother, that I didn't know who was worse off—him or me?

"Josh is just shy," Mrs. Sharpe said.

No, I wasn't. I had just trapped myself in this filthy Bolivar house, with all these Black kids staring at me and God only knows what heaped around me—guns, drugs. All for the stupid scratchboard project, the biggest damn worry in my life. Mr. Thompson was making it a whopping 50 percent of our grade, and if I failed art—and I was already failing French—then I'd fail two classes, and maybe the whole year as a result. How could I even be in this situation? No one in my family had ever been held back a year.

"Think in terms of negative and positive space," Mr. Thompson said. "Take things apart. See your environment differently. Learn to observe, rather than working from memory."

Pure torture. Nobody did scratchboard today. It went out with cave painting. If not then, with sixteenth-century printmaking. It was impossible to think in reverse for very long. Sooner or later you etched away too much black coating, and you were sunk. But there was no adding back, not like drawing with a pencil, when all you did was add.

But here I was in the worst house in Bolivar, with a bunch of Black kids gawking and laughing at me, armed with only a sketchpad. It all seemed a weird dream, like Josh in Africa or something.

To find a place to put my eyes, I looked around at the walls. I saw the negative and positive shapes reversing-the dark bookshelf becoming light, the light wall becoming dark, the whole X-ray effect again. Suddenly, out of a cubbyhole in this house appeared a girl who looked like a Black Barbie doll. Makeup, earrings, Whitney Houston hairdo. She was so pretty she looked stolen, like the TV set and Tyrone's silver trophy. Shanice! She looked so different I didn't recognize her. In school, she always wore a scarf or handkerchief over her head. She saw me and went into nasty mode.

"What's he doing here?"

Her thin eyebrows were raised up like daggers.

"To see you," said her brother, rolling on the springy bed, enjoying every bit of his little joke. He was just like my brother Jerry—a menace.

Then, all eyes fell on me again and my sketchpad.

"Josh is an artist," Mrs. Sharpe told the little ones, trying to keep the situation under control.

"I know," said Shanice. "He a show-off, too."

"I'm an artist," Tyrone said, sitting up.

He took off his cap to show me letters shaved into his afro in back, but I couldn't make out what they spelled.

"Damn, he dumb," said Shanice.

I gave her a hateful look. She might have made herself as pretty as a model, but she was still trash on the inside.

"Josh, does your mother know you're here?" Mrs. Sharpe asked me.

I nodded, and she smiled.

"She works for the town, doesn't she?"

Technically, it was for the mayor.

"They live in that big rich place with all them limos around it," said Tyrone, daring me to deny it.

He was referring to Robert Byrd's house on Ridge Street. All the little kids' eyes went wide.

"You rich?" said one of them, pulling on my finger.

Shanice was in no mood for all this chummy talk. She crossed her arms and nodded at me. "Why you here?"

"He wants to draw you," said her mother. "For a school project."

I couldn't understand Mrs. Sharpe's kindness. Her face had all the torture of slaves in paintings down in the Harpers Ferry Visitor's Center, but she went on being kind like my mother, who looked like Sandy Duncan.

"Draw me?" said Shanice.

"I know what he want," said Tyrone, snickering.

"He rich," said the same little boy.

"You here to fix our step?" said another.

I kept my eyes on Mrs. Sharpe. She was my only hope. Just then, a little fat-faced girl pushed her way in close.

"Shanice think you cute," she said.

Tyrone kicked his big foot at her, then tossed his yellow Shaq notebook at me.

"Don't look at me, Jed," he said, with another rapper's wiggle of his hands. "Draw me, brother."

He earned a few laughs for his antic.

But when I slid the chair around to see him straight on, everyone knew I meant business. Maybe I couldn't draw in reverse, but drawing regular—now that was something I could do. I opened my sketchpad, but Tyrone said he wanted the drawing in his notebook. That way he could keep it to show everyone. Mrs. Sharpe was looking on intently. Suddenly, the kids were gathered around, clinging to my shoulders and legs and breathing in my ear. One of the little ones was actually lying across my knee. It was the strangest feeling. In seconds, I had gone from a white boy to hate to someone with magic in his fingers.

I had never drawn a Black face before, except from a painting of John Henry. Not that it mattered. In portraits, every face was different. As Mr. Thompson put it, each feature was a certain distance away from the other, an exact position and relation. There were basic guideposts to follow: Between the eyes, leave space for a third eye. For the nose, start with the crescents of the nostrils. Also, remember to line the center of the mouth up with the bottom of the ears. I liked to think of it as plotting stars. Everyone's eyes, nose, and lips were like stars making up a constellation: Big

Dipper, Southern Cross, Canis Minor. The kind of paper didn't matter, and a pencil was a pencil, as long as it could be made either dark or light.

Tyrone's notebook was how I imagined his locker—full of doodles and stupid words like "bitch rammer" and "funk train"—the work of a seven-foot third-grader gone delinquent. I unjammed his chewed-up pencil from the spiral binding and put the notebook square on my lap. Tyrone, arms folded and big legs coming off the bed like toppled telephone poles, sat giving me a smug, sweaty stare. I went into my drawing mode, gazing at him for a long moment, seeing him only as the subject, not worrying about him as the big bully he was.

"You know John Denver?" said one of the little girls, leaning on me.

"He look like John Denver," said another.

To start, I needed only to get the nose right. It was slow going, drawing what amounted to BBs on the whole white page. There were no beautiful sweeping strokes, no scratchy sounds of charcoal on rag paper. My audience grew impatient.

"That don't look like him," said one of the little kids.

"I don't see nothin'," said the fat-faced girl.

"Hush up!" said Shanice.

The little girl, leaning against my shoulder, started teasing, "She like you, Jed."

When Shanice slapped her a little too hard on the shoulder, Mrs. Sharpe called her down, and that set in motion so much commotion that everyone except Tyrone, Shanice, and me was sucked out of the room. One by one, the little kids trickled back in and took up a position around me.

"Make me look like Shaq," Tyrone said, leaning forward, trying to see.

With his nose finally drawn, I could give them something to look at. In dramatic sweeps, I sketched in the cheeks and chin, to their oohs and aahs. To hell with the scratchboard project. This was what art was all about!

Shanice stood closer to me. Her little sister, with big, rolling eyes, noticed.

"She wants you to draw her next, Jed," she said.

"Hey," said Tyrone, with his mother gone, "wanna see my bullet holes?"

Shanice made a groan, and Tyrone lifted up his tank top, showing small circular scars on his fat stomach and ribs. I leaned forward. They looked like burn marks from Granddad's King Edward cigar.

"You got shot?"

"Hell, yeah. Four times."

Four times? How could he not be dead? He could see I was amazed, so he held the shirt up longer for me to see.

Shanice laughed. "You sheltered, boy."

I sat looking at her. So? Maybe I was.

"You don't live in that big fancy house," she said.

"Did it hurt?" I asked Tyrone.

"Duh," Shanice said, hitting me on the shoulder.

"He passed out," laughed one of his little sisters.

Tyrone leaned across the creaky bed, picked up a sneaker, and threw it at her.

"Get, Precious!" he said.

Half of them flew out of the room like a flock of birds, yapping and carrying on. That left the three of us.

"So you came all the way to Bolivar for a 'school project,' huh?"

I knew what she was really saying—Bolivar was second-rate to historic Harpers Ferry where I lived. The only reason anyone ever drove through it was to take a short-cut to the new highway. There were no impressive restored park buildings up there, no tourists, no park rangers, just Black families and little streets filled with shotgun houses along busted up sidewalks. Nothing historic or great ever happened there.

"He like you, stupid," said her brother.

I liked how she looked, yes. This was the first time I had seen her without her stupid handkerchief on her head.

"Did you go to Vanessa's?" I said, nodding at her hair. Vanessa's Hair Salon was the only Black hair salon in town.

"Oh, look," she said to her brother, "now the boy know Bolivar."

Tyrone, rolling out of the bed, crouched over my shoulder like the shadow of a mountain.

"You finished, Jed?"

When he saw his portrait, it was as if I had given him the world. He grabbed the notebook and ran out of the room, all his little brothers and sisters following.

"I'm gonna sell it," he was saying.

"No, you're not," said Mrs. Sharpe. "You're gonna hang it up."

I was alone in the small room for a moment. I saw a second bed in the corner, along with a sleeping bag along one wall, and another along the opposite wall. They all slept in here? In this tiny room?

Then Shanice came back in. She was strange and quiet and staring at me.

"You really wanna draw me?" she asked.

Her voice was different. All the nastiness was gone. She had the look of having worked up her courage to talk to someone who had just dropped out of outer space. What I would say next, I knew would make a fool of me. But I had always wanted to say it to a girl, and Shanice, suddenly, was the prettiest I had ever seen, even though she was Black, and somehow because she was Black.

"I know my own heart."

I wasn't sure where the saying had come from, maybe a song, but I always liked it. In this case, though, it didn't even sound like my voice. She glanced off as if trying to find the ventriloquist or something. Then her eyebrows went up. "You mean that song? Shasta Q?" When I sat there looking confused, her almond-brown eyes narrowed, and her nasty voice came back. "What you talking about?"

Before I could answer, Tyrone charged back in, acting like a clown, playing an air guitar, twanging out the Beverly Hillbillies song.

"Hey, Jed, give me an earring like Barry Bonds," he said, putting the notebook and pencil back in my hand.

"Don't call him Jed," his sister snapped.

He stopped, his expression froze up, and he started laughing so hard he fell back on his bed.

"Oh, Lordy, Lordy, Lordy, you like him?" he said, rolling around like an idiot. "You like old Jed."

"Shut up!"

"He gonna draw you? He make you white like Britney Spears." He sat up. "Know why they expelled her last year, Jed?"

"Mama!"

"Doing Mr. Jenkins under his desk."

He made a blowjob gesture with his mouth. She slapped at him, but he just covered up and laughed. As she ran out of the room, screaming to her mother, one of her little sisters came in.

"Jed, can I have a drawing, too?" she said, trying to act cute and pretty like Shanice.

A little boy came in behind her. "Can I have a car?"

Behind him was a smaller boy with a big open schoolbook teetering in his hands. He dumped it in my lap, trying to hold his finger on a spot on the page.

"Get away, Reginald," said his sister.

"Is this where you from?" he said in his little voice.

It was a map of the United States. All the states were different colors—pink, red, green, blue, yellow. He had his finger on Alabama, which was pink. I said no and moved his finger to West Virginia, which was green.

"No, that's here," he said, in a little voice of protest.

I didn't bother trying to explain that Harpers Ferry was just five minutes away. Meanwhile, Tyrone was lying on his bed, admiring his drawing. He'd be rich too if he could draw like this, he was saying. I stood up. Through the door I could see Mrs. Sharpe at a table heaped with empty Suzy-Q boxes. The rest of the little kids had swarmed outside. I could see them through the small window, carrying on in the bare yard. Shanice was not with them.

I went to the doorway and looked around. Our refrigerator at home was rusting in the same place, and we had a St. Joseph's thermometer on the wall, too. Mrs. Sharpe looked up and saw me wandering around.

"Uh, Shanice…" I said.

She had the look of a woman who understood immediately.

Behind me, Tyrone got off the creaky bed. For the first time, I noticed a trapdoor in the corner of the room and a ladder going down. Mrs. Sharpe nodded, and I started over toward it.

"You letting him go down, Mama?" said Tyrone.

I stopped and looked back, my sketchpad in my hands.

"Shanice," the mother called out, "can Josh come down to see you?"

"No!" came her nasty voice through the floor.

Mrs. Sharpe made a gesture for me to go on. As I walked closer to the ladder, Tyrone and his mother came together in the middle of the room. I felt like Neil Armstrong or somebody as I backed down the crude ladder made of two-by-fours.

Below, I could see what looked like a kind of homemade church altar—dozens of pictures of Black children on a dresser, surrounded by purple and white candles. Shanice, seeing me coming down, started running her mouth, telling me to get. Her mother yelled down, telling her to behave herself. When I got to the bottom of the ladder, she was standing back by a small bed, looking terrified and infuriated at the same time. I was glad when my hand slipped off the ladder at the last minute and I almost fell. It gave her a reason to laugh. But as soon as I started looking around at all the pictures, she started yelling for me to leave. I looked up the ladder for help.

"You just sit down there and draw her," Mrs. Sharpe told me. Then she called down at an angle. "Baby, you can show it to everyone at school, okay?"

Shanice ran her mouth about that, too. I sat down on the bottom step and put the pad on my lap. She stood glaring at me. In the strange light I saw braids in her hair and wondered how she had changed her hairdo so quickly. They made her look tough, like an African warrior. She called me a fool again, and her mother, watching over me from above, told her to get rid of her attitude.

"So?" she said, arms folded. "You just gonna gawk?"

"I need to come closer."

"So come closer!"

I sat on a stool by the dresser, out of view of everyone above. It was a small, hard, uncomfortable stool, and I sat clinging to my sketchpad, sneaking glances around. The place looked like a bomb shelter made into a bedroom, then into a miniature church. There were more cheap, white crucifixes than I could count. Slowly, Shanice sat down too. She was so light her bed barely moved. It was covered with a white lace blanket I could just hear my mother calling lovely.

"You better not make me no white girl," she said. "My boyfriend'll kill you."

I opened my sketchpad, found myself still holding Tyrone's chewed-up pencil, and went into drawing mode.

"What?" she said. "What's wrong with you? Why you looking at me that way?"

"Change...change your face."

She cocked her head. "What?"

"You want me to draw you that way? All frowning?"

With effort, she relaxed the hard lines away. From a portrait standpoint, she'd be easy. Her eyes were perfect almonds, her nose was made up of cute round shapes, and her lips were short and full.

"I can put it in a frame for you," I said.

"I don't need no frame. Just draw."

"Who are all these children?"

"None of your business!"

It was hard concentrating. Every time I glanced at her, I found myself looking at her pretty eyes. They were shining right at me. If not her eyes, her smooth, brown skin, or her braids. She had a perfect face, like one of the models in my Grumbacher Learn-to-Draw books. Why had I never seen this in school before?

"You better be drawing me," she said, "not just gawking like a fool."

I started feeling the pressure. I knew that if I didn't make her the prettiest girl in the world, she'd be the maddest. I gave her long eyelashes and lips perfect from corner to corner. Each line and tone had to be right.

"Why you here? You like poor people?" she said. "You ain't gonna get no money for this."

"I know."

I had no answer, and she made a sour remark about that, too. Then she burst out laughing.

"You like Jenny Wilt?"

I tried to act annoyed.

"Yeah, you do," she said, her face filling up with a giggle. "Jed and Jenny."

"Shut up."

She was surprised that I could be just as sharp-tongued as her.

"You're a trip," she said.

As I glanced at her and drew, I could see her studying me back, making her own portrait of me in her mind.

"Why you act all lonely?" she said.

"What? I don't act 'lonely.'"

"Yeah, you do. Like a lonely little dog."

I called her foolish and tried to keep working.

"You scared of something, boy?"

"Shut up!"

She laughed again, then started humming, trying to distract me.

"You don't recognize that?"

I stopped, a blank look on my face.

"Duh, 'To Know My Heart,'" she said. "Shasta Q? Damn, you dumb."

I went on drawing, ignoring her little putdowns. I worked on her lips, her high cheekbones, the bridge of her nose, adding tone and sharp lines. As hard and nasty as she was on the inside, she was prettier than any white girl I had ever seen.

"Now," I said, sitting up, "how do you want your hair?"

She hopped up off the bed.

"You mean, you can draw it the way I want!" she cried out.

She opened the dresser behind me and started pawing through a heap of wigs-straight brown hair, straight black, brown curls, purplish curls, blonde.

"Turn around," she said.

I stood, pencil and pad in hand, and turned around.

"Okay," she said.

When I turned back around, she had on shoulder-length braids. They made her look like an Egyptian girl.

"What?" she said, not liking the look on my face.

She told me to turn around, which I did. A second later, she had on even longer braids, like strands of beads hanging from a doorway. I shook my head.

"Why?"

"'Cause they're for a round face."

"Round face?"

She sighed and gave me an irritated look.

"Okay, turn back around. Damn, you hard to please."

This time when I turned back around, she had on some wild hairdo flipped out at the bottom. I shook my head, she sighed even louder, and back around I turned.

As I waited, I had a chance to look at her bedroom. No posters or pictures of teen heartthrobs. Just pictures of children surrounded by unburned candles. Over her bed was a simple wooden crucifix. It reminded me of my mother's bed.

"Do you know all these kids?" I asked.

"None of your business. Okay, you can look." I turned around. She had on a long shag.

"Better," I said.

"Better?"

"Something shorter."

She cocked her hips and, with a displeased look, made a little looping motion with her finger for me to turn my back. I didn't understand why she didn't want me to see her changing wigs, but she was being fussy about it.

"Are they relatives?" I asked, my back to her.

"No. Okay, you can turn around."

This time she had on a wavy, collar-length bob she called a bouffant shag. I didn't like shaking my head, but it wasn't exactly right, either.

"Damn, boy!"

I assumed the position and stood looking down at her bed covered with beautiful white lace. I thought she must look like a princess sleeping in it.

"Are you a 'big sister' or something?"

"Why you like Jenny Wilt?" she asked back.

"She and I were born the same day."

"That ain't why."

"What?"

"Don't turn around!"

I wondered what she was doing that took so long.

"You a virgin?" she laughed.

I was not too scared to tell her to fuck off.

"Yeah, you is. Okay, you can turn around."

"No, I'm not either—what's that?" I asked, looking at her latest wig.

Right away. she didn't like the look on my face. "Motown side part—you better like it, boy," she said.

I stepped over to the drawer as if I owned the place. She watched in amazement as I reached into the drawer of wigs myself and picked out a short, dark, curly wig.

"This would look better," I said. She gave me a suspicious look. "Why?"

"Cause your face is ..."

She crossed her arms. "My face is what?"

"Oval." I waited for her to get nasty, but she didn't. "This'll show more of it," I said.

She gave me a long look.

"Where'd you learn that?" she asked.

I told her about my art book at home, in which it explained how different hair styles complemented, or didn't complement, the face. She burst out laughing, saying I sounded like one of those funny men in hair salons.

"Virgin," she called me again.

"I am not."

"Yeah, you are."

"No, you are," I said.

To that, she gave me such a smug grin that I knew it couldn't possibly be true. It made me sad. I was hoping she was.

We went through a dozen more wigs together. Spiky bangs. Wispy bangs. Bangs plus waves. Wet look. Sassy look. Two-tiered shag. More shoulder-length braids, and even a wild red wig for fun. She had wigs showgirl long, others ooh-la-la short. Even something she called a "face-framing, cascading straw-curl cut," which I thought looked like a big blonde pompom. She was going to be a model, she said. She would need all these wigs in her career.

"You been to the museum on River Street?" I asked.

It was the only way I knew how to say Black History Museum without coming out and saying it, which I didn't feel comfortable saying. She looked at me as if there was no such street. She knew someone on Potomac Street. But she had never heard of River Street.

"They have a famous"—I was careful to say exactly right—"Afro-Americans gallery."

She cocked me a look. "Afro? Whitney Houston there, too?"

I didn't get what was so funny. Speaking of Whitney Houston, she had three of her wigs. She showed me. I shook my head to all three.

"This one," I said, pointing back to my original choice.

"Short shag? You wanna see my dumb ole face, don't ya?" she said, hands on her hips, wig balled up in her hand.

I nodded, and she made the turnaround motion with her little finger. After a few seconds, she said I could look—and boy, did I look.

"Oh, stop getting all google-eyed, boy. You don't have to look at me like no fool."

Her face flashed happiness, embarrassment, confusion, and anger. Some of these looks were wigs, too. I just didn't know which.

"You failing?" she said. "I bet you are. They gonna hold you back a grade."

"I'm not failing."

"Yes, you is."

"I'm failing art," I said.

She stopped and looked at me. "Art? You? For real?"

I didn't bother with trying to explain. I sat down on the stool again.

"Damn, don't get all sad about it, Jed," she said.

She was so hard on me, I almost wanted to laugh. At the same time, the irony was bending in me. She was the prettiest girl I had ever seen, and I had picked on her for years behind her back. And to think, now I was liking her.

I thought of my mother, seeing me down in this bomb shelter of a bedroom on Union Street, playing with a Black girl's wigs. I could see my brothers behaving no better about it than Tyrone. I saw every white girl in my school looking at me as if I was doing something to offend the race. Why was I turning my back on the timeless rite of liking one of them instead? The answer was simple. None of them liked me.

"Wanna come down to the museum with me?" I asked Shanice.

She cocked her head. "You and me, boy? Just walking right down the street? Like we married?"

"My brother will drive us."

"I ain't gettin' down with you," she said, crossing her arms.

My face blushed so hard it felt hot. I had never heard it put this way.

"I know," I said.

She stood looking at me. "You know?"

I never expected myself to be so agreeable about something that was so far down some impossible road anyway. She gave me a look of curiosity.

"Why you all nice?"

When I shrugged, she shrugged back, to make fun of me.

"Then you'll go?" I said.

She looked off.

"If you ask, maybe," she said.

I hopped off the stool and practically leaped through the ceiling.

"Damn, you weird!" she shot back, trying to hold back a smile.

Weird was good. Weird, in this case, was her funky red wig. I reached down into her drawer, grabbed it, and draped it over my head.

"Get that off!" she said, snatching it back and trying to act mad.

I picked up a black wig and plopped that one on my head instead.

"Look, I look just like you," I said.

She stood there shaking her head. I held a blonde wig above her head.

"Now you look just like me," I said.

She grabbed it away from me.

"Hey, what about my drawing?"

She made me sit and start drawing again. As I worked, giving her perfect hair, I could feel her looking me up and down.

"Why you white boys so short?" she asked. "People gonna look at

us in school."

I turned to her.

"Hey, does Mr. Romine really live in Bolivar?"

"I don't know. Now, why you failing art?"

I had no answer. All I could do was shrug. For that, she stood looking at me, head turned to the side.

"You poor?" she asked.

"No!"

"Then why you wear those old shoes? And those ratty pants?"

"Why you wear that stupid shirt?" I shot back, pointing at her oversized black buttons.

"You act poor, boy."

"Shut up!"

"Ooh, SEN-SI-TIVE about it, ain't ya?"

She turned and looked off.

"Least you have 'self-confidence.' Ms. Kerry say I lack it."

"No, you have it."

She turned back to me, surprised I had said this so automatically. I didn't even know what self-confidence was at that moment. I just wanted her to have what I had. Then, as if I had given her self-confidence, she stood, stepped over to me, and touched my hair. She started smiling, saying how soft it was. She had never touched a white boy's hair before. She stood there for some time, too, pulling every lock to its end, her thin brown arm over my head, blue bracelets clicking together and making a tickling sound in my ears. If my body had been the St. Joseph's thermometer upstairs, I would have burst.

Then she looked down at my drawing.

"Wow, that's me? How'd you do that?" she said, leaning down beside me, her wig touching my neck.

I gave her a little demonstration. With the side of my pencil, I shaded an area of her cheek, then rubbed it with my finger, blending an even tone.

"It's like you putting makeup on me or something."

She squeezed onto the stool beside me, not shy about letting part of her touch me. She had perfume on, which made me think of some far-off place.

"Put some here," she said, pointing to a spot on her cheek.

"No, it has to be natural," I said.

"Here."

The graphite on my fingertip made a soft tone across her forehead. If I had been drawing a white face, I would have left the area white. Suddenly, she took hold of my hand and turned my finger up to see the pencil graphite on the tip. Then she looked over my whole hand, as if looking for the magic in it.

"You'd be rich doing this," she said.

"That'd be nice," I said, my voice dropping off. She looked over.

"You are poor, ain't ya?"

"Kinda."

Her forehead pulled up in soft wrinkles, like ridges in the sand.

"Over in fancy Harpers Ferry?" she said. "For real?"

I nodded and looked around the basement. I was the only white face in this room, in this house, and on this street. Maybe the only white face in this whole town. That meant my little white secret could come out. My family probably had the worst house in historic Harpers Ferry—run-down, embarrassing, and hickish. Ordinarily this was no big deal because there were always Black people in Bolivar to put down first. But with me here and with all the whites across town, lies didn't matter. They were like a suitcase full of Confederate money.

"So where do you live?"

I braced for impact.

"Hog Alley."

"Hog Alley!" Her voice shot up. "You're kidding? Which house?"

"The yellow one."

"Down by all them boxcars and that huge pile of coal?"

I nodded, and she shot to her feet.

"That place with no windows?"

"It has windows."

"No, it don't." She jabbed her finger into my shoulder. "That place is a dump!"

I laughed so hard that, fearing that the whole house had heard me, I scrunched down and put my hand to my mouth, acting all silly.

"That's a nasty old house, Jed!" She pushed me off the stool and onto the floor-sketchpad, pencil, and all. "You're a snob, Josh Connors!" She started pinching and poking at me, and I was laughing and trying not to pee myself. "My mother got cancer, and you all looking down on people," she said, digging into my stomach.

"What?" I said, pushing her hands away and sitting up. I was trying not to laugh now. I climbed to my feet. "What, Shanice?"

"Ovarian," she said in a low voice, with a glance toward the ladder.

I took half a step closer.

"Serious?"

She nodded.

"She seen three specialists already."

The planet stopped turning, the house went dark, and my mind folded down to one thought: death. It wasn't about Harpers Ferry or Bolivar anymore, or whose house was nasty-looking, and it certainly wasn't about art class or even whether I'd fail for the year. The worst part of all, it wasn't even about her mother's cancer, either, which it should have been. It was about how mixed up we both were and how every little thing less than death always ended up being more devastating to us.

Then Shanice did something incredible—she threw her arms around me. It was a strong, beautiful hug that squeezed my shoulder blades so hard my arms popped out straight. As quickly, she let go, sat down on the stool, looked off in the opposite direction, and, with her arms draped over her knees, started rocking herself back and forth. When I took too long to put my arm around her, she smacked at me. I deserved that. How to touch someone when it really mattered—this was something my brother's dirty magazines never taught. And the only time my mother ever touched my father was when he wanted Caladryl on his back.

Tyrone didn't know about the cancer, she said, sniffing. No one at her church knew, either. Her mother only told her because she was the oldest. As I sat listening, the moment seemed unreal, and I was trying to catch up. She broke into tears, but her voice rose up in rage just as quickly.

"My mama already had one surgery, and now it's back!"

I told her my grandmother had three surgeries, but every time the cancer came back.

I had another chance to hold her, but again my arms were lame. When Shanice turned to me, glassy-eyed, I knew what she was thinking: She may have been poor and Black and from Bolivar, but she knew how to put her arms around someone when it mattered.

When I said that maybe her mother would get better, she said that less than one percent survived after the second surgery. She said that some girl at school had a cousin who died in a hospice after three surgeries and two years of chemo.

I watched her step over to her bed, sit down on it with a bounce, fall over on her side, and curl up like a child. I started toward her, but she popped up first.

"So why you come here?" she asked one final time, taking a step toward me. "You never talk to me in school."

I didn't like her icy smile or her tone. She knew very well why. Because of my stupid school assignment. That, and what I told her earlier.

She shifted her mean little hips again.

"Oh, you just come up here by yourself because you 'know your own heart'? No other reason?" she said, flouncing past. "You as disgusting as me."

"What? You're crazy!"

"No, I ain't," she said, rounding her bed and bouncing down on the other side of it. "You disgusting, and you know it. I know your house now."

"Stop calling me 'disgusting'!"

I stood glaring at her for the longest time, then turned away. Thousands of kids blurred in my eyes. White crosses did zigzags in the air. She was right. I was disgusting. I didn't feel good enough to set foot in one house over in Harpers Ferry. Not one! I had searched every street before coming here, looking for just one door to knock on. I walked past fancy house after fancy house, not feeling worthy of approaching one. I ended up two miles up the road, where people wouldn't look down on me.

Slowly, I walked back over to Shanice and sat down on her bed with her.

"So I guess we're in the same boat," I said.

"No," she said, throwing my arm off her, "you in a worse one."

She hopped up and pulled her shirt down snug, saying she hoped she didn't get cooties from me. No telling what she might pick up from my ugly old house over in Harpers Ferry.

I was back to glaring again. Nothing worked with her. Not kindness. Not anger. As soon as I thought something was happening between us, she blew up in my face. I couldn't tell her she was pretty. She'd only get angry and slap at me. I couldn't tell her she was an angry bitch. She'd slap me for sure then.

"Your mama raised you," she said. "That's your problem. Made you like a girl."

That was one hell of a remark even from her.

"I was sick when I was younger," I said. "Okay? It's not my fault."

She looked back at me.

"Sick?"

"Almost died."

"For real?"

She started closer. I had set up something dramatic. I had to deliver, and that wouldn't be easy, considering her brother had been shot four times and was still alive.

"Fever. 108."

"108!"

"Almost caused brain damage," I said.

She came over and sat back down beside me. Her little brother Germaine was sick all the time, too. Fevers, earaches, colds. He spent a whole week in the hospital once, she said.

I spent two whole weeks in a hospital in Baltimore. The nurses gave us Curious George books. We watched Joe Bazooka boxing movies. I was in a large room with all kinds of sick kids—blind kids, kids with no arms, kids with cancer, all of us mixed in together. The kid beside me had no legs, I said. His name was Win. I thought that was strange. The unluckiest boy in the world named Win? He bothered me the whole week, asking me to unlock the combination lock on his luggage.

"I still think about him."

Shanice looked at me as if I was the most pathetic kid in the world.

"You too shy," she said, feeling my curls.

When I looked at her, something in my face disappointed her again. She stood and stepped off.

"Why you all that way?" she said, looking back, her face all strained up.

She didn't know the half of it. In the picture window of the wax museum across the street from my house stood a big figure of John Brown, all done up in fury, thrusting a musket. All our lives he had been glaring at our house. We always figured he was enraged with our racist father. In a town famous for being where Black freedom started, Dad was begging for it.

"I guess we all a little poor," she finally said. "You have a phone?"

"No."

"Me neither. TV?"

"Yeah."

"We do, too."

I picked up the notepad, sat, and started working again, with her quietly beside me. I wanted to tell her she was easy to make beautiful on paper. She was already beautiful. All I had to do was copy her.

"He looks like my cousin," I said, pointing at the picture of a boy on the end of the dresser.

"What, you have a Black cousin?" she laughed.

His name was Anthony McDonald, she said, standing. I stood with her, and together we stood looking at the pictures. There must have been fifty.

"They all kids killed in Anacostia this year," she said.

"Anacostia?"

"Southeast, D.C."

I could guess how—drive-by shootings.

"You ever light these candles?" I asked.

"I want to," she said. "But Mama say I'd burn the house down." She pointed to a little girl missing her baby teeth. "That's Shanice. Her name Shanice, too."

Standing beside her, I could hear the happiness in her voice. Shanice was a cool name, I said. All the girls down in Harpers Ferry were named Sarah or Emily.

"I go by Shani to my friends," she said.

"Shani," I said.

I pointed at an older boy in a suit.

"Who's he?"

"Brandon Carr."

She named the two boys beside him, Luther Washington and Justin Mennefee, then went on naming them by their first names—David, Kayla, Jasmine, Destiny. I looked over at her. She had a strange, peaceful smile.

The names went on and on—Briana, Ashley, Michael, Anthony.

All these smiling little faces—a boy with a ball cap, a girl our age, another toddler. All Black and all dead. All dead as if because they were Black. Suddenly, I felt very tired, and a sick feeling ran through me. I had to sit down.

"Now what's wrong with you?" she snapped.

"Nothing."

"Why you all red-eyed?"

"I'm not."

"You don't know them."

Still, I was sad, so sad I had to sit down.

"You asked me who they was," she said, getting upset.

"I know."

I glanced back at the ladder.

"Go ahead, leave."

I wanted to. I wanted out of this basement funeral home, this mausoleum. How could she sleep down here with all these dead kids looking at her? It was as if she was trying to be their mother or something, when her own mother was dying from cancer. It was too morbid to stand.

"Ain't my fault they dead," she said, getting more upset.

I was weird, she said, and her boyfriend was going to kill me for being down here, and she wouldn't go with me to a museum if I was the last boy on earth.

"My mama the one dying!" she all but shouted, her face raked down to the bone in anguish, pictures of dead children ringing her.

"I know," I pleaded back.

"Your mother should talk to my mother."

She looked tripped up by this and let out an ugly laugh.

"Your mother?"

Yes! After dealing with our grandmother's illness for years, my mother could talk cancer the way I could talk baseball. All of us, even my stupid brothers and hard-ass father, after seeing Grandma turn yellow from cancer and the skin fall off her bones, would have the hearts of Mother Teresa for this family.

But Shani wanted to fight more.

"When your mama ever come over into Bolivar?"

It was hopeless. There was too much garbage between us. All I saw was Black, and all she saw was white.

"Your mama think we're trash," she went on.

"So don't act like it."

I caught her hand coming for my face just in time and threw it away like balled up paper.

"I hate you!" she hissed.

Just then, Tyrone's big, dark arm came down from above, yanked off her wig, and disappeared up the ladder with it. She screamed and tried to cover her head with her hands, but not before I saw the ugly white scar across her scalp and the mangled hair growing around it. I couldn't take my eyes off it. It was the ugliest sight—hair and white skin smeared together as if her head was made of melted wax. And where there wasn't a scar or messed up hair, there were pasted-down cornrows that made her head like a boy's.

She screamed at me to stop gawking, stomped her feet in a crazy fit, all while trying to grab another wig from the drawer. But she ended up putting on the funny red wig, which made the moment worse. She shrieked for me to get out, threw the notebook at me but hit her dead children pictures instead, scattering them on the floor like cards. Then she really went berserk, flailing her arms, whimpering. I stood petrified. When her mother yelled down, wanting to know what was going on, I went on autopilot.

"No, it's okay, it's okay," I called up, doing my best to sound calm. "I'm not finished yet. It's okay."

I looked over at Shani and put my finger to my lips. She stood backed up against her bed, half angry, half confused. I picked up the pad and pencil, sat down on the stool again, and started erasing. Before she could scream out that I was ruining her drawing, I put my finger to my lips again. She quickly put on another wig and started gathering up all her precious pictures and putting them back in place on the dresser.

"Shani?" her brother called down.

"Get, Ty," she said, her wet eyes transfixed on my hands.

"You okay, baby?" her mother called down.

"Yeah," she said, in a distracted voice, stepping closer to see.

The best thing about Tyrone's stupid, chewed-up pencil was its big, soft eraser. Spinning the pad on my lap like a piece of pottery, I quickly erased her hair. Keeping the lightest pressure, I was careful not to rough up the texture of the paper. Several times I stopped to blow the paper clean and to turn the eraser to a fresh side. Out of the corner of my eye, I saw her coming closer. I knew that since I looked like an expert, she wasn't having another conniption.

"It's okay, it's okay," I kept saying, smiling and nodding.

My heart was pounding for the life of me. I was scared of her, but embarrassed for her, too, and crazy about her all at the same time. She drove pain into me, then pulled it out like a hammer clawing nails out of lumber.

With her hair erased away, I started drawing in cornrows. Another girl in my class had them, so I knew just how they looked. I built little rows of rounded lines. I worked quickly, too, not sure how long I had before she would go crazy again or her mother would call down. Where she had her terrible scar, I drew in full, dark, beautiful braids, flat to the scalp, in perfectly spaced rows around her pretty face. Out of the corner of my eye, I could see her peering over my shoulder.

"Don't make 'em too thick," she said.

"I won't," I promised.

She sat down beside me again.

"How you do that?" she said, sniffing.

"I don't know," I said.

"Talent," she said, answering herself.

"My father painted when he was younger."

She looked over.

"But you ain't close to your father?" Her voice was different—light and weak from her little spell.

I shook my head.

"My father hit me," she said.

I looked at her. I couldn't dare kiss her. I couldn't even say something sweet. All I could do was wish.

"Put more here," she said, pointing to a spot.

I nodded and laid the pencil on its side and gave the paper an extra shot of tone. She was tired of wearing wigs, she said. She had to wear them for the rest of her life.

"When?" she said, sniffing.

I looked at her. Her face was relaxed, and she was gazing at the drawing with wonder.

"When what?"

"When are we going? I can go tomorrow—wait," she said, turning to me on the little stool, "what am I gonna see?" She sat with her arms crossed, as if her little fit had left her chilled.

"Paintings," I said.

She looked disappointed again.

"Any pictures?"

"Some."

"Least they got that," she said. I could feel her looking me up and down. "Why you wanna go with me? You can't hold hands with me or nothing."

"Maybe not in public," I said.

If she could feel my hand, then I could hold her hand. I stopped drawing and took hold of it. It was soft and small. I touched one of her long blue fingernails.

"You're silly," she said, sniffing. She saw me look over at the pictures. "The church gives them out. I just started collecting them. Somebody got to remember them. You gonna let go of my hand?"

On the edge of her bed was a six-subject Mead notebook as thick as a dictionary. I had seen only one before. The smartest kid in our school carried one.

"Can I look?"

She nodded.

With its deep blue cover and embossed silver logo, it was the opposite of her brother's flimsy notebook with a goofy, canary-yellow cover. On the inside cover was "Shanice L. Sharpe, Harpers Ferry High, 10th Grade."

Underneath was a poem:

*Someday I'll fly like the bird I cannot see. Someday I'll love like the heart I cannot feel. Someday I'll smile like the face I have not seen.*

Lights were sparkling in the corners of my eyes, and my body felt like a hot air balloon I couldn't keep down. With all my heart I wished I was Black, or she was white, or we could stay down here forever.

"Your mom miss your grandma?" she asked.

I nodded. Life, I thought, was not scratchboard, but finger-painting with a hopeless mess of gruesome colors. You kept smudging it around until you got it right.

"What kind of cancer she have?"

I couldn't remember exactly, and that seemed to disappoint her. She looked down at her notebook on my lap.

"Ms. Kerry say I have self-esteem issues—why you smiling like that?"

She was why I was smiling. A UFO could land on my head, or my scratchboard project could hang in the National Gallery. And my first girlfriend could be Black.

"You can be a model," I said, "if you have the guts to do that."

I nodded at the shrine of pictures on her dresser. If she could collect pictures of dead children and sleep with them staring at her all night long, then she was the coolest, bravest person I had ever met. She could move anywhere, become anyone. I told her so, and all anger went out of her eyes.

"You serious?"

"If you can do that," I said.

She looked down.

"I've never been to a museum before," she said, looking down.

I shrugged. It was okay that she lived in Bolivar but had never been down in Harpers Ferry. I had lived in Harpers Ferry all my life but had never been here, I said. She didn't seem to hear, though. She was looking down at the drawing of her with perfect cornrows.

"I know why you draw."

"Why?"

She didn't answer. She just smiled and put her head on my shoulder. I stopped working, and we sat still. Seconds stretched out into minutes. Sometime later, there were footsteps above.

"Baby," her mother called down, "we going to the new Piggly Wiggly. You and Josh wanna come?"

Shani turned her head up to the ceiling.

"No!"

Silence came back down at us. Long seconds of it. I could feel her mother peering down at another angle, trying to see what we were up to. We sat perfectly still on the stool, holding hands, our fingers making sweat in the crevices.

Shani then exploded on her.

"Yeah! He still drawin' me, okay?"

It was a boom to put an end to all nosy mothers. Then she looked at me, grinned, and put her finger to her lips.

"Okay then," her mother said, moving off. Then she stopped. "Goodbye, Josh. Say hello to your mother for me."

I let go of Shani's hand, went to the ladder, and looked up. "Goodbye, Mrs. Sharpe," I called up.

But she had already moved away, and all over the house, kids were running in circles, shaking the floor. Doors were being slammed, and Ty was causing trouble. He yelled down to us—"Hey, Jed, don't do nothin' I would do!"

The first time the big galoot was funny. But Shani didn't smile, just told him to shut up. More door slamming, more house shaking, more squabbling. Finally, after a stampede down the outside steps, shaking the whole rickety house like a treehouse—quiet. It filled this basement room and settled on all the picture frames like the tranquility of evening time.

Wigs lay everywhere as though Shani and I had flung off our clothes in great passion for each other. Finally, through the old boards of the house came the sound of a car with no muffler popping to life. As it pulled off, she and I sat looking at each other. Around us, the walls rose up with a glow from upstairs. It made me think of a night sky over us.

She scooted closer and sat with her legs under her.

"You wanna see my nipple ring?"

As I nodded, I felt her eyes hook into mine. I watched her unbutton her shirt, her thin, dark fingers climbing down the front like a spider. She lifted her moon-white bra over one breast. It was small and brown, and the ring on her nipple, catching the light from above, was a gold angel inside a sunburst.

"Ty's lying. I ain't been with no boy. Not the right way, anyway." Her eyes were as big as …. "You can touch it," she said.

She rose up on her knees and leaned over me so that her breast was directly level with my eyes. Angel, nipple, and breast bounced like a Christmas tree ornament to the touch of my finger. I didn't have time to get excited or think about what I was seeing and doing.

"It's beautiful," I said, looking up at her.

Her eyes were a thousand glints as she opened the last remaining buttons of her shirt. Her confidence was raw and pure. Speechless and powerless under her gaze, I wanted what she had.

# Memory of Distant Friends

My new marriage kept me in New Hampshire for two years without a visit home—a trip to Boston, another to Montpelier, but not home, a Civil War town in West Virginia, not seventy miles from Washington, D.C. At night, when Ellen dropped off to sleep, I lay awake wondering why I was painting houses in Londonderry, forty miles from Boston, when I could do the same in Whites Ferry, my hometown, where lucky Skeeter still lived.

Lucky, because during my years in New England, my childhood friend Skeeter still saw our hometown every wonderful day—the historic antebellum homes along Shenandoah Street bearded with thick ivy, the see-through shimmers of green, marbling the rivers that converge at Whites Ferry, and the massive stone piers of the trestle bridges, layered with frosty-neon graffiti. Every second of every day, he delighted in this scenic, charming town in the foothills of the Blue Ridge. He still lived in this fable.

He still peered up at the fog-veiled cliffs. He still ventured through the gaping hole in Brown Mountain, the giant cylinder through solid rock, the train tunnel my grandfather helped to dig in 1903. He still rambled the narrow cobblestone streets past the restored yellow stuccos and the bottling works, rebuilt for historic show after bombed by the South, strewing chunks of cobalt-blue glass for generations to uncover.

How I envied Skeeter, staying in a simpler, innocent time. During the helter-skelter of city life, I imagined Skeeter far away, his arms outstretched like a plane as he drifted down the slope of the old Catholic cemetery, hopping roots and rocks along the Eight-Tenths-Of-A-Mile Path. Lucky, because he still climbed Split Rock, seeing far downriver where the Potomac effortlessly blended with the Shenandoah River like a wide, level sheet of algae-wrapped glass.

We laughed at our dizziness as we crossed the gapped planks high over the Shenandoah River on the Valley Line walkway, splintered and unsafe. Lucky Skeeter still smelled the melting creosote on the black iron trestles.

When I last saw Skeeter, he was no longer lucky. He was stuck dead in time, trapped in those moody, wasteful years after high school. He languished at a crossroads, looking for his future. His hair had thinned so that his head already had the late-thirtyish look of his father. His face was sallow, and he himself seemed encased in a stage of life. He could not find his passion and purpose, a commitment to a profession, his adventure to test his favorite book in his life, *The Unbearable Lightness of Being* by Milan Kundera.

During these five years of sporadic weekend trips from college in Boston to my childhood town of Whites Ferry, I occasionally asked Skeeter, in the language of two young men uncertain of their independence, how he was inside, in his heart and mind.

Answering lightly, he shrugged and said, "Okay, I guess."

He was not okay, and our relationship had already weakened since high school. Even if I had heard any encouragement from him to reunite us after high school, the cycles of semesters at college and my series of bank teller jobs along the bottlenecked routes in Boston separated us by engrossing me in the life of an urban professional stuck painting houses. Even when we tried to act irresponsibly young and boyish again, even when we hinted we really missed each other, time no longer wanted us together.

On the Sundays I visited, while Skeeter and I hiked the firetruck trails outside Whites Ferry, he'd bravely ask, in a fragile pitch, "You goin' back tonight?" By asking this question, he'd bring up the nostalgic whims of the moment, as if reminding me that I, not he, had left town first.

When Skeeter finally met Ellen, he was managing a Comfort Inn at night and living across the road in an apartment for older folks, where all old people my mother had known eventually went. During what seemed an awkward introduction at his apartment door, I sensed, as did Ellen, an exchange of goodbyes. Skeeter was leaving my heart. Over the winter, he had grown a small prim mustache, browner than his hair but thicker, hiding his womanly mouth.

While Ellen and I waited to be invited inside, an unfamiliar and intensely vital man appeared in the bathroom hallway, inviting his own introduction. Skeeter never mentioned a word to me of what seemed more his experiment with homosexuality than a lifelong propensity, the very words I chose to defend him needlessly to Ellen. She drove us home, the weekend by my command shortened.

As the Blue Ridge maples opened into horse pastures, then highways and concrete curbs and Shell stations, Skeeter, I realized, with his fascinating change of life, had told me of his private choice for male companionship and for me to stay away, to live at a distance. His happiness seemed as normal as mine, though perhaps more endearing, delicate and deserved.

Ellen taught second grade in Boston a year before we moved to Concord, where she managed a geologic specimen store. Soon after, she become part-owner, a trusting gesture by the other owners in Boston. She stabilized us since my business degree had not benefited us. In truth, I had discovered how little college had taught me and, as long as Ellen wanted, she could carry us.

In Concord, she walked three blocks to work while I rode in the back of a truck to paint residential windows. As long as she could stomach my job, I could. Ellen cherished each new moment. She loved the capital city, the darkly varnished Colonial houses, the lighted steeples. Petting the bossy Rottweilers and silly, unguidable Labradors each day in St. Paul's Park, Ellen soon wanted a dog of her own.

Francis, a black Lab mix, had lived on our front porch in Whites Ferry for eleven years, breaking his chain and escaping constantly. When he turned eight, as if his mind had started deteriorating, he blindly rammed his muzzle into parked vans along the Shenandoah River. The crunching buckle and popping recoils of door panels created a spectacle along the cinder lot. Park rangers never once caught Francis. Forever spastic and frothing, he darted into cars and tourists alike and, given a chance, would gleefully run himself dead chasing me, choking on his own foam. His lonely wail at night always sounded personal, so I tried sneaking him into my room. But his paws would patter through the pine floorboards, and, excited, he'd tip a chair or desk, alerting my mother.

To her, Francis lived a tragic life.

"That poor dog needs a friend, so he can just run and run and run," she'd declare whenever chaining him after a walk, her hands red from the tugging squeeze of his long leash.

I was Francis's friend, I thought.

While irked by his relentless barking, she pitied his existence at the end of a chain, relieved only by his brief, controlled trips to the river in the evenings. In the bitter winter, he'd curl himself on burlap in his dog box, and in the mornings, he slinked outside for breakfast—breakfast gobbled, barfed, and regobbled. In my mother's time, all dogs except poodles stayed outside. Dad wanted his brat kids to stay outside.

Before school, in the years while Francis still looked young and cute, I'd stand on the top doorstep and wait for him to emerge from his box, hearing the links of his chain slide across the threshold of his particle board box. When he saw me, he smiled with straight, undamaged jaws, I was sure, and when I jumped and called his name, he shuddered his black glossy body in joy, ready to run and run and run.

By talking to him and tickling him into sheer elation of attention, I briefly forgave myself for his horrid, chained-up life. My gibberish soon formed a verse. Stroking his body, I'd say, as if in his voice, "My name is Francis. I have an alligator head and red marble eyes. I have a Lab body, thumping tail, and I like to shake hands. I smile and like to lick faces."

He'd nearly convulse in happiness, but when I started toward the bus stop, he'd erupt into barking, furious at being abandoned again.

A year before he died, my mother and I rarely walked him, and when he barked at tourists wandering down our street, we rapped the glass, embarrassed by his misshapen muzzle and infected eye, green with disease neither of us had the courage to address. Dad had left Mom by this time, and my stupid brothers were now older, stupider bothers wasting what they made as welders on big trucks and pricy apartments.

With his chain tangled and shortened, poor Francis wallowed in his own turds, which I neglected to bury. His hair collected in the water pan, sometimes found dry. The amounting smell and clustering horseflies soon forced me to leave the house by a back door, in shame and disgust. Each morning, sitting on the school bus, I'd quietly beg Mr. Penwell to gather speed on the hill so that we'd pass my house before Francis could bark at me again for leaving him.

Then, overnight, bloated in his box, Francis died. I took the task of burying him, though Mom appeared beside me with a tarp in which to wrap him. Tourists were gathering and watching from across the street. Dislodging him from the dog box proved difficult, and when Mom went inside, choked by the sudden stench, I yanked savagely on his chain, creasing his neck and springing his legs through the opening, his body rolling free. More than once, I heard joints pop.

Carried through the house, his first time ever inside our house, Francis lay in my arms, vulgarly stiff, eyes open, legs bouncing, his neck still chained. His long black hair, shedding even after death, stuck to sweat on my arms. When I had managed to carry him up the bank and into the backyard, my mother was crying behind me. I let him fall, disgusted. Mom, abandoned by Dad, had lost her will. I was generally miserable. Nonetheless, the shame of his mistreated life had left us before weeds had sprouted over his fertile grave.

Gentle, faithful Ellen said that whatever I regretted from childhood, I would amend as a father. Her conviction for my well-being always seemed not only angelic and divine but also remotely destined, as if as a girl she had witnessed my painful years in real time. She was a strangely close woman, insightful, informed, a kind of postponed guardian.

Marrying her had seemed more a personal comfort than a declaration of romance. Romance without the chaos of emotion had become to me a distant, failed pursuit.

Aletha was an oily Milltown girl. In junior high, she and her older sisters would all meet in the hall downstairs where they clannishly moseyed to the next class. They were distinguished in name only by the length and shade of their plastered-down hair. My hair, as short as peach fuzz, emphasized the ghastly oblong shape of my head—shaped as if carrying an extra cavity of brain, a humped growth that others gaped upon in disgust and amazement. Kids said I had lay on my side in my mother's womb, and that accounted for my squished, Martian-like head. Thin and nervous and dressed in Acrilan vests or itchy turtlenecks, I endured the years in genetically gypped defeat.

Happy to have any boy near them, the Milltown girls in my class eventually flirted with me, and although I tried to appear disgusted by their vulgar gestures of a love affair, they secretly pleased me. Aletha, the best of them, known for her premature breasts, would smile desperately from her corner of the classroom. In the light from the window, her finely graded pimples, colorless under a layer of beige makeup, reminded me of my own fragile disfigurement, my oblong head, which she seemed more than willing to overlook. The class snickered, catching us passing notes, yet they applauded us, too. Our shared mortal flaws made us an endearing couple—beasts finding mates.

Aletha came to Whites Ferry one Saturday, on a senior citizens' bus, a van-like diesel called the PanTram, costing an automatic sixty cents to anywhere in the county. In the daylight, Aletha looked coarser, her pimples and lantern jaw more pronounced. From a distance, with her hair braided, she looked like her brother, who suffered in the grade behind ours for his height.

"You live here with all these tourists?" she asked in a manner making me as illustrious as a boy whose family owned the limestone quarry where her father ran a digger.

She had spoken loud enough for her raw Milltown twang to reach one of the pastel-colored crowds in town from D.C. for the day. She never saw the glances at her, more indignant than curious. Embarrassed of her, I walked her into a remote area of the park, then farther from civilization. I hopped the rail fence running alongside the closed Valley Line trestle bridge.

"I'm not going over that," she declared.

From her smile, I realized by her reasoning I had begun to court her. She had written me love letters and let me slide my desk near hers, and now she had come to see where I lived.

As I pulled her to the top rail, one of her pink sneakers hooked the post in a queer, upright angle, and she fell forward, her knees leaving deep impressions in the hard chunky gravel. From her courageous resilience, popping up as if she had crossed the fence without incident, I knew she fell like this most days.

She followed me to the river as if coming home with me, and along the driftwood path, in the leafy breezes and sunny openings, where no one could see us together, I reconsidered her as a girlfriend. I absorbed her shape, her energy, in my environment, confused when, in certain natural gestures, she looked pretty.

We relaxed enough to sit together on a rock along the bank where, staring beyond the sunlight, we watched cars leaving town in the afternoon. They filled the passenger bridge as reflective blocks above the green grid of the railing.

"Sure a lot of people here in the summer, I bet," I heard her comment.

Grape-colored scrapes had surfaced on her knees, the skin there grated in parallel lines, only now filling with blood. I glanced at her, repelled again by the pimples, the red bumps and blotches, harshly visible in the glistening sweat. As if revealing an item of wealth or beauty, she showed me a thin scar curving between her breasts, which she expertly kept under her sweater, an old scar put there by her brother, she delighted in sharing with me.

Eventually, as the minutes breathed in the breeze, our loathsome standing in school, pardoned for a moment by the glorious sanctuary of nature, returned in unredeemed bondage. Ultimately, by my own reasoning, I felt superior to her. I told her to walk herself back to town and stepped away from her, into the woods, turning and running when she stood to follow. Bewildered and quickly angered, she chased after me but proved too slow to catch me. Offering her no explanation did not occur to me as selfish or cruel at the time.

When I had outdistanced her and sat on another rock, safely canopied by sunlit, translucent green maples, I removed my cap by habit, a stiff railroad cap. Feeling the cool air mold the shape of my head, I realized that she, too, had taken a chance coming here and being seen with me, with my alien-like head.

A decade later, at a party not far from town, I heard her name mentioned by a stranger whose plastered hair, which I had noticed several times during the evening, at once matched those in my memory of Milltown. Mine, blond and feathered, I kept blow-dried and long in the back to hide the shape of my head from the world, even from Ellen, or so I thought.

Aletha, I learned without arousing association, married some local and had gone to work in the quarry office, typing, answering the phone. This evening, standing in the incessant traffic to the beer keg, I thought of her outcome. Later, when Ellen and I crossed the passenger bridge at Whites Ferry, heading back up north, I glanced down at the dark, pluming riverbanks, realizing why I had left.

My reason for staying in New Hampshire, however, had changed. Last night, as Ellen gave herself a stomach-ache from too many vanilla cookies, I went on our evening walk alone for the first time since moving to Concord. The familiar, narrow sidewalks and lighted shapes on the side streets moved quickly behind me. Stopping when the walk ended and the cinder shoulder began, I noticed I had gone beyond the thickly painted bed-and-breakfast Victorians and brownstone villas behind St. Paul's Church to the tree-embedded bungalows on Kay Street. Ellen and I had never ventured this far on foot, as staying close to the house was a precaution we had started when living in D.C. Here among the sporty cars and sweet oleander hedges, I realized I had nowhere, other than back to Ellen, to go. My job as a housepainter was not rewarding, but the clean yards and small windows around me appeared as lasting, wonderful components of our new home, this town.

Ellen and I planned to go to West Virginia next month for a week or so, as she had found a reliable part-time girl for the store. But, standing here, stopped beside the hedges in the darkness, I knew we had no reason to go there, the town here alive in us with an exciting memorable tingle.

# Missing

Her small, photocopied face, hopeful of a rescuer, never
stops staring with perky and untouchable teen beauty—the
look probably killing her—from the corner of the Missing
Persons poster. But every face not made of paper says to
her, "You're dead already."

Likely so, for in the vast, cynical, and hot-tempered world,
at least one person could take her life, a bleak and heartless
logic.

Still, a paper face never dies, and, staring into a Nebraska
shopping mall far from where she went missing, she cries
for help, pleads for it, and implores more searches for her.
Though, we all know she's beyond hope, missing for fourteen years, missing longer than the life of the sun-bleached
blond boy passing her poster right now. Ahead of him on
this Friday evening are two whole days without classrooms,
an eternity. As paper, Jane Doe, too, has eternity ahead of
her, too.

To those glancing at her, she stares from the tattered
poster and into the present, to identify herself as not missing.
She shouts out to the world on this clarion morning at this
dusty Midwest mall where her body lies as an entangled
matter of bones and threads from the sweatshirt she wore
that swift, swift day.

Hers, a brutal and sad and unpunished crime, people
think, shaking their heads, gripping their children tighter,

walking away and forgetting a face depicted here too young to identify now anyway.

Jane still lives on the poster, where she neither ages nor decays, nor can she frown or cry. Someone murdered her, maybe strangled her with the long purple sock she wore fourteen years ago.

"Jane was last seen walking to a friend's house along Washington Street in Beaverton, Green County, Virginia," the missing person poster reads in condensed pica type. The serifs looked struck to the paper in hopeless anger.

If alive, Jane is thirty-one. If dead, she lived from seventeen years old to perhaps a moment ago. This loose range of her life upsets anyone glancing at her toneless, black-and-white graphic face, a face now probably only a skull. But when she was seventeen, her cheeks were rosy and jubilant about seeing the world through her mother's Instamatic.

At this moment, Jane stares at an old man caught in a conjoined gaze with her. His black Lab, sniffing the brick front for her scent, perks up. The old man wonders, could she really be alive? He searches his life since the September she vanished. In the blur of changing neighbors, the advent of husbands and grandchildren in his family, the August picnics, the countless rotations of weeks and seasons, all coming to him like a spin of frames on a filmstrip, he admits—doubtful. So he moves on, but his Lab stretches the leash, still sniffing as if dogs can see ghosts.

Jane's unknown fate hurts too much to feel and accept. So few people stop. Instead, they glance long enough not to recognize her, much less to acknowledge her. Like those movies jumping back in time, she lives on the poster, when in fact she stays lost under fourteen seasons of leaves rotted from rain and snow in a culvert beside a highway. There, the salt for snows on the road has seeped down to her. No dog has dug up her leg and trotted happily home.

What of her father and mother? Any co-habitual lean toward booze? Undercurrents of blame and visits by the reverend who, except for the picture of Jane still on the mantel, cannot even remember her face. Or the bedroom her mother has entombed—the drawn, yellowed window shade, the cold, flat sheet tucked tightly over the slim mattress, the one sunken pillow positioned memorially. Hope from the tomb.

Jane's sister? Brothers? Do they still search for her, trace leads and write newspapers?

Who got her? Her abductor is unimaginable, abstract, and shapeless in the infinite and reticent shades of each person passing her poster. Jane ought to be complaining about her weight and the onset of crow's feet. In the evenings, she ought to be cleaning up trails of limp nightshirts, juice glasses, milk rings, and dropped and trampled storybooks.

Instead, she exists as composite parts of photocopier carbon, black islands on amorphous puddles of white paper, together forming a basic semblance of her. She was seventeen, 115 pounds, with her fragile blonde hair bundled into ambitious motherly curls, festive and infectious. She stares with almond-shaped, expectant eyes welled with rambunctious blue.

Yet what of her play friend who had set out to meet her that black September day? Does she, once a little girl with Jane, on an eerie afternoon alone, expect the old black rotary phone with which she had lasted talked to Jane, a phone too sentimental to discard, unplugged and boxed in the attic, to ring from the grave?

Hurrying up the steep stairs to the attic, she answers the phone and hears Jane in a thin and distant voice, spanning years. Jane says she will come over later. They can go into town, take the bikes if nice outside, and sit on the porch of Slatter Grocery where Johnny Link stops on his new motorcycle, its black metallic black seat so groovy. Johnny always carries a spare helmet on the back of his bike. He needs a girlfriend, Jane teases, licking a melting fudge Popsicle, her mouth ringed with sooty, sticky sugar, looking like a coal miner.

"Jane, where've you been? I've been waiting for you," her friend says into the unplugged phone. She sits on her knees beside a cardboard box in the attic, fourteen years later. "Come on over." Her voice is girlish, how they both sounded at that age. "Come on over, Jane."

# Electric Church

Moving into a vintage home on Historic Hill facing the grand Georgian church awaits them as the greatest event in their young marriage.

"There she is!" says Michael, stepping back from the window.

The church stands just across the street from them in the waning afternoon light and rises three times taller than any other structure on the island.

His exuberance with the church excites her; she's not only resourceful but also romantic. All at once, she kisses him. In a second kiss, she notices a glimmer rising up the church tower in the summer's twilight.

"There she goes!"

Over the next few minutes, the steeple and evening sky exchange light and dark. As if the sky were a planetary globe with an adjustable light, the evening dimmed that the steeple could illuminate without throwing a tungsten and halogen tint on the floating summer clouds. Like the imperceivable movement of a minute hand, the increasing light can't be caught with the eye or with the breath. It dawns behind the middle pilaster of the arcade and the shallow sill of the Palladian window. In a rising flame, it encircles the archways and climbs the ridged planes of the spire, advancing past the golden steeple to the weathervane.

At the same time, sharp lines of electric-orange streak along the balusters, shoot up the pinnacles, and scatter in a lambent glow inside the arcaded belfry. Dimension deepens quickly, flawlessly. The gold ball on the Staff of the Righteous glows copper. The entire tower, in short order, illuminates over Block Island.

Michael and Ellen watch, silent and fixed. He doesn't notice the coffee placed on the table for him. She never made hers.

"It's so neat, honey! Isn't it?" She locks hands with him. "Remember when we came down here during the snow?"

For him, the sporty tone she uses, while associating them with the church, reaffirms the proximity of their apartment. He answers her by flicking her a well-pretended grim face.

On those slushy, wintry nights nearly a year ago, when they'd treat themselves to a view of Historic Hill, they'd schlep ten blocks from the public parking lot to stand beneath this steeple. Descending snowflakes as soggy as bits of wet tissue peppered their upturned faces. Then, they'd traipse around the church, down unlit, abruptly ending side-walks, through a pestilence of watery snow puddling in the ancient streets like lime Slurpees. So entranced by the tower, they sat on waterlogged bench slats, marveling at the surreal, hypnotic effect of the lights.

"Beautiful!" Michael says of the display.

Ellen points broadly to an area of the carpet where the imposing steeple stands entirely visible.

"Let's put the bed there, so we can see it before going to sleep."

"Sweetie, think, we have this perfect view outside our window, all to ourselves, for a whole year," he says.

When he leans to kiss her, a bluish flare in his peripheral vision, as intense and instantaneous as a camera flash, throws her face into shadow. Puzzled, they both peer down into the street, seeing umbrellas of light misting from the street poles, an undisturbed scene. She then notices the steeple, the absence of light on the left side of the tower.

A blown bulb?

Neither speaks. The angry triangle of shadow has swiped the pinnacle and most of the balustrade and belfry with blackness. They turn to each other, horrified.

"Shouldn't we call someone?" she asks.

For him, the elapse of seconds slows miserably to intense mental blips. The instantly lopsided light upon the steeple has destroyed an entire corner of the ornately stacked symmetry of the tower. The steeple is now offensively misshapen, compositionally ruined by an unfaithfully expiring bulb. For them, a dozen stars winked out.

Ellen proposes dialing the rectory of a church and alerting someone. Michael dreads a week of nights will pass before the caretaker climbs through the arcade with another floodlight, a vast week of a dark church.

"Well," he sings out, turning and walking to the kitchen with an overcompensating stride, "there's more to this place than its view."

Ellen keenly doubts the prompt ease of his tolerance. She senses his extinguished spirit. The steeple is an overpraised, inflated, grandiloquent idol neither of them needs. To hell with it.

"Honey"—she feels the coolness of his absence—"they're probably calling the church right now."

Keys jingling, he calls from the front door, announcing he's getting the coffee table out of the car.

"Now?"

With the table in hand, he turns through the doorway, steps, turns again, and mounts the wineglass staircase with a

Formica coffee table from Goodwill. He's careful not to nick the fluted wood column. Once on the top step, he glides the table down the hallway, raising it above the iron handrail, a technique he had mastered earlier with soft-cornered boxes.

Then, things fall apart. When he rounds the portico, he bangs and hooks the table legs on the narrow rails. The pointed legs dig into the dense oak pillar, and when he steps back, his rump bumps the door of the landlady's apartment. The metal sleeves and coasters on the table legs rattle. He despises this cheap and flimsy, wood-grain table, laughably light but still clumsy.

Upstairs, in the apartment, when the church bell rings loud and close, he cringes from the obnoxious sound.

"Do we even know why they light churches?" Ellen asks as he slides the coffee table into the darkest corner of the room.

"God after hours?"

She smiles for her comedian.

# Pictures

Loving Liz required of him a peculiar and almost distasteful custom her mother had started, a maternal tradition cutely called "Pictures."

The idea was, with his index finger, he'd lightly draw endless blobs and wiggles and loops on her back, to put her to sleep. Awkward and uncomfortable with his technique and skeptical of any pleasure, Mark tried to convert Liz to neck and back rubs, himself sure of these comforts.

Nope. Pictures. She insisted on them.

"This is weird," he said, as his insensitive finger left red figure eights in the trough of her wintry-white back.

"Too hard!" she said, eyes opening.

Lying prone, with her teddy bear nightshirt hooked over her neck, she took his untrained finger, repositioned it upon her skin, and ever so lightly swirled his hand until he resumed with precise pressure and speed.

The wilder the better, he soon learned. Her precise instructions betokened how seriously she regarded the practice. He was wary. The notion of his replacing her mother with this odd bedtime tradition bothered him. He wanted no part of it. Secretly, he wanted no association with his mother-in-law.

"Mommy used to do them for hours," his wife would say whenever he tried to quit after five minutes.

So to love his wife, he kept his finger swirling.

Like a baby in a crib, Liz soon asked for Pictures every night and refused to sleep until he glided artful shapes from a fingernail, all of which she had filed and smoothed beforehand.

"No, honey, not tonight," he insisted. "I'm tired."

Her babyish fits of pounding the pillow and kicking the mattress, amused him at first, but soon became troublesome. They forbade a mystery in her behavior. A problem.

"Honey, please. I just can't sleep without Pictures," she pled.

Her girlish cuteness ultimately defeated his reluctance until, within months of their relationship, she kept him cross-legged on the bed for an hour.

"No more!" he announced.

She rose in protest.

"You've had enough, Ms."

By now ambidextrous, he had mastered the technique, remembering to bring the squiggles and scrawls up the neck every few minutes, and, as long as the TV entertained him, he even appreciated the rhythmic and continuous swaying of his arm, a meditative sensation of blind finger-painting.

Still, he could not imagine the pleasure, why his inkless and shapeless drawings felt so good, so sensual and relaxing.

"Please, just a few minutes."

Nagged into continuing, he invented positions—he on his side, she on hers, then both overlapping—until he discovered lying on his back. With his body perpendicular to hers and his arm outstretched, he could whirl and swirl and curlicue on her back without discomfort.

This position, other than her occasional complaint of the blunter point of the thumb, satisfied both of them until, once again, she rose and whined whenever he stopped, even if he outlasted the David Letterman Show.

He stopped and sat up, sullen.

"How long did your mother do this each night?"

He knew to expect an outrageous answer, but hoped to rectify this so-called game, now more cruel than cute, more sinister than absurd. Queerly evil, he thought.

"I don't know. It felt like all night." She jerked her thumb for him to continue, adding, "And they weren't sloppy Pictures either."

Her demanding manner gave the task an ugly taste.

"That does it, Liz. No more."

Hurt, she ignored him until he apologized, and seeing him tame again, she incorrigibly chanced, "Pictures, please, for a few minutes."

He touched his finger to her warm back, and, with heroic swoops, shaped his best Pictures—gentle, varied, constant— and when he had melded momentum and style, he, too, risked.

"Better than your mom's?"

Her answer made his night a private conquest.

The next evening, ill-fated for him because of late coffee, insomnia struck. Mark tried walking the neighborhood, glasses of water, cough syrup, shower, bowl of cereal, a book, standing and pacing, whining to Liz, begging God, and, finally, lying on the floor.

"Here, I'll rub your back."

Her offer reminded him of the months since she had last massaged him. Her hands felt weak now, diminished by the day, without the vigorous kneading he wanted.

"Not hard enough," he complained.

She tried again.

"There. How's that?"

"More."

"Honey, it's late."

"Please."

"Okay. Let's try this…"

Lying there on the carpet, in the bluish condo tint of the bedroom, he felt at last her fingers become a single point, a fingertip suddenly sketching Pictures on his back, wiggling, arching, constructing a trail of sensations too haphazard for thought, confusing him into sleep.

# Short Lives

The little cemetery of tilted slate markers appeared alongside the road before them, behind the varnished split-level homes, just as their conversation had soured, and the complaints of their first year of marriage quickly yielded to the seriousness of this place.

Stones, some merely the unengraved bases of the original upright marker, weaved and leaned and toppled in semblances of rows. A few stones were so small and shapeless they appeared as a natural part of the knoll. One headstone, chipping in fibrous clefts around its ball-like corners, had weathered so that only the baseline serifs remained. The tops of letters wavered in faint depressions as if drifted with sand.

He stooped and strained to read the stone, scoured for centuries into a coarse texture of artful incurvations, some spotty from bleaching. But he recognized only isolated letters of what itself appeared to be a venerably composed epitaph. At the top of the upright stone, uneroded concurrent lines of scrollwork neatly filled the contour of three converging circles. His wife, still huffy for some reason, said represented the Christian family—the father, mother, and the child.

A child. He wanted to wait for a few years. She wanted a son now.

To discover this picketed family cemetery, she walked away from him, meandering until finding a stone whose letters, facing those patiently obliterated by a ceaseless breeze coming off the inlet, had stayed thin and dark and defiantly deep. The houses behind her, lit for dinner, looked cheap and recent and trespassed on the cemetery, he thought, following her.

Leaning down, she read the inscription aloud when he arrived, conscious of the soft earth, the young wild grass, each endearing antique stone.

"In memory of Deborah, second daughter of Nicholas Partington. Died"—her voice fell—"died twenty-seven years of age."

Surprised, he remarked on the short life, feeling the ground give when he shifted his feet.

"Probably of consumption," she guessed, standing and walking away, to rebuke him slightly.

He stayed to study the letters—finely striated and ribbed during chiseling—and the numbers in slate, chronicling the interrupted span of her life, a life stopping at the age he had become last month. The moment grabbed a fierce edge of mortality. The timetable of her brief life—the arrival and departure of dates narrowly separated by what looked like an intentionally shortened dash—quietly upset him. Sitting in uncut grass, he reread the spiritual phrases and with his fingers followed the grooved outlines of petals and stems. His wife watched from a few steps away.

"Not very old, was she?" he said once in the car with her.

He waited for her to respond. But she had no words, her silence akin to the seriousness of this place.

# We Never Liked Them Anyway

Mom and I heard the weather report first thing. The storm had dumped more than a foot on the Eastern Panhandle overnight, closing schools in Morgan, Berkeley, and Jefferson Counties. I tore off for the closet for my galoshes while "Bob in the Morning" continued with the county news:

"The Leetown Fish Hatchery has announced plans to expand its Jefferson County facility..."

Mom went on ironing, her body doing a little shimmy as she worked the iron back and forth.

"Josh, keep your boots snapped up today," she called out. "Remember what happened the last time?"

Mom was still pressing my flannel shirt when I hurried back with my boots on. Every time she set the steam iron down, it hissed. When she picked it up again, it gurgled.

"...in other local news, Harpers Ferry Park Superintendent Ronald Wilkinson faces sexual harassment charges by two park employees. In an internal investigation, the employees alleged that Wilkinson used sexually offensive remarks repeatedly over the last several years. Local businessman Lee Jackson, outspoken critic of the park..."

The iron hissed like a serpent, covering up the next few words. Mom's face, in the steam, looked as hard as copper.

"...calling for his resignation. An investigation by the EEOC is scheduled for next month."

Mom planted the iron down. I could see every one of her forty-seven years whittled out to the end of her nose.

"There must be some mistake," she said. She turned to me. "Did he just say Ronald Wilkinson? He did, didn't he?" She stared off into the light of the room. "My God."

Just then, "Bob in the Morning" let loose with his famous hyena laugh. His timing was terrible. Mom pivoted and walked out of the room. In the kitchen, she put her hands on the table as if all she could do was to hold herself up. When I came in, she was sitting down, pretending to look at a postcard.

She looked up.

"*Our* Ronald Wilkinson?" she asked again.

* * *

My mother loved him the first time she saw him. It was a winter morning three years ago, and she was on the front porch, feeding our dog. She looked up, and running down the street in the snow was a man in red long johns, smoking a cigar. Jogging for exercise, in long johns while smoking a cigar! He had wild copper hair and a smiling, rugged face and a big sturdy body bouncing around. In a hearty voice, he called out hello to her—by name: "Morning, Mrs. Connors."

As Mom stood there gaping, he gave her a second wave with his cigar hand. The look of astonishment stayed on her face for hours. That was our new park superintendent? That was Ronald Wilkinson?

Not once in the thirty years the National Park Service had been in Harpers Ferry had a superintendent ever said hello to my mother, much less made spectacle of himself in the street. Our last superintendent was Marvin W. Phillips III from Annapolis, Maryland. What a perfect snot he was. He lived in a big house on the hill and came out only to whisk around town in his sprawling new car. He waved to no local, certainly not to my mother. He had a chalk-white daughter no one liked, either.

The situation in Harpers Ferry was this: my mother had the last privately owned house in the historic part of town, and she was refusing to sell. To the chagrin of the park, our house was an eyesore. The mortar was crumbling, the windows were cracked, and paint was peeling. Basically, the town was getting famous for its role in the Civil War, so it didn't want locals tarnishing its handsomely restored image. But this very attitude had my mother on her ear. Our house was how it was supposed to look, she said. There was nothing wrong with the natural, rustic look. It was a matter of taste. It irked her something fierce that when park rangers passed her on the street, they wouldn't even nod and most of the time looked past her as if ashamed she existed. She expected that treatment from tourists, but not from the people in authority.

In the first few months under Wilkinson, the park hired local women for administrative jobs. That never happened before. My Aunt Helen applied but wasn't even thanked for her effort. Also, under Wilkinson, the park maintenance crew took on local boys for the summer. Mom said I could apply in a few years. Marty Howell became a full-time ranger—the first town native to do so. It was good politics all around.

My mother's heart was beaming. For years, driving home meant leaving behind the little community of white houses that surrounded the town hall and entering crowds of tourists from the city. The first cuss words out of her mouth came at the end of the day when she pulled up to our house to find tourists leaving Coke cups and wrappers on our front porch. Now, when she went home and saw Adam and Mike Wilkinson carrying on in the street, not caring what the tourists thought, it made her grin and remember when she was young, before the town became a tourist trap, and she played on the hill. It came down to this: If the superintendent and his family could act like yokel locals in the historic part of Harpers Ferry, why couldn't we?

*  *  *

Mom stood and finished ironing my shirt. The words were all over her face. Sexual harassment?

"Have you heard anything, Josh?" she asked, her voice strange and soft, the way a bruised apple would sound if it spoke.

When I shook my head, she looked off. At the same time, Bob's hyena laugh returned. She set the iron down, marched over to the radio, and turned it off with such force the whole box slid to one side, revealing dust to be cleaned. Briefly, I saw the bones in her face coming out.

Shocking! Filthy! She would never listen to that station again, she declared.

"Oh those poor boys," she said, looking off into space as if seeing into their home, seeing Mrs. Wilkinson, Mr. Wilkinson. Then she turned to me, bent down, and said, "Josh, whatever you do today, keep those boys away from the radio."

This was circa 1970. TV stations in the city couldn't reach us here in the mountains, no matter how many times and whichever way we turned the stupid antenna on the roof. Local news came by way of town hall, the bank, and the school, all of which were closed due to the weather. That left the radio station WXVA, in Charles Town, a few miles away.

Snow day or not, keeping Mike and Adam Wilkinson away from any radio would be easy. We were never indoors anyway. We had a whole national park to play in.

An hour after snapping up my galoshes, I found Mike and Adam down at the railroad tracks, hammering the sides of a slow-moving freight train with heavy wet snowballs. I looked closely at the two of them, searching for any sign that they knew about their father's shameful situation. As brothers, they were opposite. Mike, three years older, was good-hearted. Adam, my age, was sneaky and mean. This morning, both were as simple-headed and happy as ever.

We horsed around for a while until they turned the snowballs on me, and it became a game of chase. As I led them across the train bridge into Maryland, in my mind, I was taking them out of range of WXVA, which I imagined stopped at the state line, at some great invisible wall. At the ruins of the Salty Dog Bar, which had been painted white by the park and looked almost invisible in the snow, I started climbing up the mountain.

\In the light snow, I could see a million white flakes falling over the perfect dark hole in the mountain that was the train tunnel. I pulled myself up from tree to tree, the wet snow peppering my face, and worked my way around outcroppings, not stopping to look down. Soon, I was in the mist and fog and light snow where eagles and hawks rode the currents up and down like elevators. Mike and Adam's shouts were faint and far below.

When I reached the main face, I ran out of trees and jagged rocks to hold on to. That was always the problem. No one ever made it beyond this point in the winter. Not only did I come to a stop, but with nothing under the elbow-deep snow to pinch onto, it took all my strength just to hold on. Still, I could feel the earth pulling me outward. I imagined Mom coming out on the front porch to feed our dog, looking up, and seeing through all the snow across the river the little blue spot on the cliffs was me.

Mike was yelling up from a ledge some twenty feet below, telling me to come back down. Below him, about the same distance, was Adam, and below him, still all the way down on the train bridge, was Ron-Ron, their disabled brother.

I had one chance. I swung myself to the side, slipped hard against the rock face, and dropped about ten feet, then tumbled and rolled until landing on my butt in an outcropping of deep snow. My old snap-up galoshes popped open and instantly filled with snow. If these cliffs over the tunnel at Harpers Ferry had been Mount Rushmore, I would have just landed on Lincoln's nose.

"Man, Josh," said Mike, picking me out of the snow, "what's wrong with you today?"

"Nothing."

"Something is," said Adam, grinning. He was standing back and had his devil face on as usual. He wanted to see me break my neck.

Mike said we should head back down. For that, Adam called me a pud. That was how it always worked between the three of us. The nicer Mike was to me, the meaner Adam got.

I started climbing sideways, pulling myself over tree by tree. Mike shouted down to the road to tell Ron-Ron to meet us on the fire truck road. The snow on the side of the mountain was knee-deep, so by the time we reached the fire truck road, my jeans were wet all the way up and the insides of my galoshes were clamping my feet in hard slush. In the road, where the snow wasn't so deep, Mike and Adam saw my busted open boots and wet jeans. They were both wearing nice brand-new snowsuits and high zip-up boots. Mike looked worried, and Adam looked happy.

I took off running up the fire truck road for the cabin at the top. Soon the snow was so deep I had to knee my way through. Adam, excited about seeing me freeze to death, was keeping up. Mike was yelling out that it wasn't funny anymore. Ron-Ron was just making his way up the far turn.

The woods back here were quiet and undisturbed. There were birds on the snow-filled branches, and cold sunlight came down in rays like in a painting. As I ran, I thought about what Mom had said—keep them away from the radio. I was taking them about as far away from the radios in town as anyone could. I also thought about what we had heard. Sexual harassment? It seemed a strange accusation, as if the words didn't say what was really meant. There was flirting, which everybody did, and there was rape, which nobody did. This was something in between that nobody knew exactly what it was. I had seen most of the women who worked for the park. It must have been the blonde one who always wore a tight green skirt. All the rangers looked at her. I tried to image Mr. Wilkinson saying something wrong to her. I couldn't—he was married and had a good family.

On the steep incline over the creek, I fell face-first in the snow, twice. The second time, I hit my chin against my knee, dazing me. By the time I hauled myself into the cabin, I could hardly feel my feet anymore. When I stomped around on the floor, it felt like I had peg legs. Outside, Mike was calling out, his shouts muffled by the heavy snow. His big shadow came through the door and leaned across the bare cabin floor to me.

"Damn, Josh," he said, seeing me shivering over by the cold fireplace, "what's wrong with you today?"

"Nothin.'"

"Don't say 'nothin.'"

He gave me a concerned look. He knew I was growing up without a father or brothers, and that made me a sissy.

Adam came in behind him, panting and grinning. He had never seen anyone near dead before. Ron-Ron came in next. Snot was running down his nose. The three of them stood looking at me, their breaths coming out as white as fog.

"His crazy father's come back," Adam said.

My father was crazy all right. Everybody knew that. But he was never coming back. He had lost his job at the electric company because of his drinking, and that was that.

I kept stomping my feet on the floor, trying to get blood back into them. Adam was looking at me with a snarl to his upper lip. He hated how weak I was. It drove him crazy that I could be like a girl and stand myself. He whipped out his bowie knife.

"Hold 'em!" he said. "Need to amputate the feet off a damn local!" When he made this voice, he was imitating somebody crazy, like madman John Brown. Or maybe his father, since Mr. Wilkinson had a raspy voice. It always made Mike laugh, and that was all the encouragement Adam ever needed.

Ron-Ron, like a battery-powered Frankenstein, grabbed me by the shoulders using just enough force, and Adam pressed the shiny blade against my leg. I knew he was pretending because Mike was still grinning. As long as Mike wasn't concerned, neither was I.

* * *

The first time I saw Mike, I loved him the way my mother loved his father. From my window, I had been watching him run the Stone Steps near the church. There were 68 steps from bottom to top. He ran them half a dozen times without stopping. Then he came into our backyard, gulped from our water hose for the longest while, and let out a belch that came clear through the three-foot stone walls of our house.

My mother looked around and said, "What was that?"

Later, he came to our door and said he needed me as weight on his back. He was going to carry a 110-pound barbell—the whole Montgomery Ward weight set—up and down the Stone Steps, and he needed extra weight to make it a challenge. All the way up and down, as I clung to his sweaty back and he stumbled over the steps and tourists gawked and pointed, he burst out laughing at how crazy we must have looked. I thought that was the coolest, how he could work so hard at something but take it lightly, too. Even while he was wheezing like a horse, nearly dying, it was funny to him how he appeared to others. I had never seen that in a person.

I had also never seen a father and son like Mike and Mr. Wilkinson. After karate class on Tuesday nights, they usually sat together in a ranger jeep, waiting for Adam. They were the same size in the shoulders and the same height even when sitting down. As they talked in low voices, they looked like big friends. They reminded me of the profiles on Mount Rushmore, because even when they were looking off at different angles, they seemed to fit together.

* * *

Adam was pressing the knife harder against my leg, daring me to take it. The last time he got carried away like this, he jabbed me in the hand with a pencil and said it was an accident. Then he stabbed me in the other hand and said that was an accident, too. Thanks to him, I had matching black dots on my palms from where pencil lead had broken off under my skin. A girl in my class said I looked like Christ.

When he turned the blade point against my leg, it cut in—I flung my arms and cried out until Ron-Ron let me go. Rubbing my leg, I looked over at Mike. With his psycho brother around, he never stuck up for me. But when just the two of us camped out in this cabin, he didn't stand over in the corner, embarrassed of me. It was our house then. We arranged the metal cots in front of the fireplace, brought in firewood from outside, then sat around eating Doritos and bouncing on the cots until bored enough to hike down to the cliffs and pretend to be Civil War soldiers shooting at the town.

Adam flung the knife at the wall, sticking it in.

"Damn locals," he said in his John Brown voice. "They lie!"

I shot him a look.

"Lie about what?"

I quickly turned to Mike—he was glaring at me as if things between us had changed long before today. They did know about their father!

"Ron-Ron," said Adam, "say 'Josh fell off a cliff.'"

Ron-Ron said it back in his weird, fast drone, and Adam burst out laughing.

"'And now he's nothing but a big red stiff.'"

"Nothing but red stiff."

"Lie about what?" I asked again.

Mike wouldn't even look at me.

"Why don't you toughen up, Josh?" he said, kicking through leaves in the corner of the cabin for kindling.

"Why don't you get a life!" I shot back.

This is not what I wanted to say at all. Something was all wrong. Adam was egging us on just by being here.

"Your mother should have remarried," Mike said in all seriousness, scooting a burnt stick into the center of the floor.

"Well, your father shouldn't run around in his underwear."

Adam was excited. Mike and me arguing?

"He's a puss. Kick his ass," he laughed to his brother.

The worst feelings were swarming in me as I looked at Mike for a truce.

"Damn, don't cry about it," he said.

"I'm not crying."

"Crying, lying local," Adam laughed. "It's because of his mom. She babied him."

My head whipped up in anger, and I lashed out.

"I heard about your father."

I kept my eyes on Mike. It was between him and me. A shiny, embarrassed smile broke over his face. For a second, he actually looked scared of me.

"That sexual harassment thing," I said just as smugly as I could.

Adam was too scared to know what to do, and Mike was just standing there, not so proud anymore. The great Mike ashamed. It was exciting bringing Mr. Decathlon down to size.

"Ron-Ron," I said, "say, 'Dad with a stiff one'."

"Dad with a stiff one," Ron-Ron said.

Adam, switching sides, burst out laughing, and Mike didn't know which of us to tell to shut up. The great Mike taken down a peg. For the first time, I had leverage. If I couldn't have a good father, neither could he.

He turned and shoved his brother for starting it all, sending him down in the snow dragged in on the floor. In the scuffle, Adam ended up near me, and when Mike came at both of us, Adam and I were out the door, running up the fire truck road together. It actually felt great to be on his side for once.

All the kids called him a psycho because he was always doing crazy stunts, like running his sled into gravestones. He was also a bully and a rat. The first time I hung around him he busted me in the mouth in a game of touch football. As I ran home to Mom, trying to hold back the tears, Mike came along to make sure I'd be all right. Adam tagged along for just the opposite reason—to see me cry. Whenever I glanced at him, he had this excitement on his face, as if seeing me crying was the best thrill in the world, better than the dead body he supposedly saw in the back of the funeral home.

Mike, as it turned out, wasn't chasing us, so at the top of the hill, Adam and I slowed down. His crazy grin was wearing off, and he started looking uncomfortable. He never liked being alone with me, and he seemed to be remembering that now. I was too much like a girl for him, the way I talked about feelings all the time.

When we came to where the road forked off onto a blue-blazed leg of the Appalachian Trail, he looked back to see if his brother was following. My feet weren't cold anymore, I told him. Not that he cared. If I loved Mike because he reminded me of my brother, then I hated Adam because he was like an old kicked dog you couldn't trust. The trick was to act friendly, then work behind his back.

"When my dad cheated on my mom," I said, "she was crazy for days."

I thought he would tell me to shut up, but he glanced over, looking worried. Without Mike around for him to try to prove himself to, he had this scared look that made his face skinny.

"She move in with your grandma?"

I nodded. Adam knew my grandmother. She was the woman always telling him not to run over her flowers.

"You think your father's gonna be transferred?"

It was either hit me or answer me. He had lost his edge, and I had gained mine. I knew what he was afraid of. When he first came to Harpers Ferry, he was too small for his age like me. That was another reason he did crazy stunts all the time, to make himself stand out. If his father were transferred, he'd have to start over in another town, and chances were, another town would be nothing like Harpers Ferry. There'd be no cliffs for him to hang from, no rivers to act like Tom Sawyer in, no tunnels to let a train chase him out of. He'd have no way to stand out.

When he shrugged, I said, "Yeah, moving would suck."

Mike could read my tricks, but Adam was a dummy. A dummy with people and a dummy in school. In the hall at school, he would flip his textbooks over to hide the covers so that no one knew he was in Phase 3, which was for below-average students. He was so afraid Ron-Ron's disabled brain was in him, especially because he looked so much like him.

I started jogging, making him follow me for once. "Yeah, my mom's all worried about your mom," I said.

His mother, it was well enough known, had a mild heart condition. I wanted to remind Adam of that. He stopped again and looked back for his brother.

"He'll catch up," I said. "Come on."

At the top of the mountain where the trees thinned and the snow had drifted, we reached a level stretch on the trail.

"I wonder why they call it 'harassment,'" I said, slowing down.

Adam grabbed girls in school all the time. He and his gang did. Sometimes they took it too far, pinching and grabbing from all sides, all of his buddies at once.

"Remember Kimmy Grove?" I laughed.

He always gave it hard to Kimmy. He thought nothing of grabbing her right between her legs and fingering around for a good long second.

"Remember Marianne Childs?" I said.

Supposedly he had sex with Marianne in her pool. When she and her parents left for vacation the next day, he brought everybody by for a look at his "gysum" he said was still floating in there. I thought it was soap scum.

We came to a tree across the trail. Adam sat down on it and looked down at his shiny boots in the snow.

"Peg Wilt," he said in a weak little voice I hadn't heard before. "She called the house." He reached down, picked up a stick, and winged it into the trees. "Mom went crazy."

"Peg Wilt?" I said. "Piggy Peg Wilt?"

He looked up at me. I was grinning. Peg Wilt was nothing but a local. She had one of those GS-7 administrative jobs that didn't pay well and that the park gave to local women out of pity. Mr. Wilkinson and a local woman? I couldn't wait to tell Mom.

"Man, Peg Wilt," I kept saying, grinning and shaking my head as if there was no tomorrow for his family. If Peg Wilt was one of the two park women, then the other one was probably a local, too. "Did your mom catch him with her?"

I wasn't scared of him anymore. He was like something wounded and on a chain, too. He looked over, too dumb to figure out I was making everything worse.

"They're talking about jail time," I said.

He looked up. "Who?"

"The guy on the radio."

He got an angry look, as if he was going to beat up the guy on the radio. I snickered inside as I walked around behind him, seeing how small and slump-shouldered he looked. He started saying that he didn't want to move, that his father had messed everything up. He was pathetic, Mr. Tough Guy suddenly talking like me, after picking on me for the same reason all these years.

I picked up a clump of snow that had a stone in it and threw it at the side of his face as hard as I could. It exploded against his face, and he went reeling off the log. But he bounced up as quickly, all wild-eyed, ready to kill. I pretended to be scared, then pretended it was an accident, saying I was aiming for his shoulder. He stood ready to punch me, but instead flung off his glove and touched the side of his face. When he saw blood on his fingertips, he was more angry, then more scared. Seeing him weak and helpless was the best feeling.

"It's just a scratch," I said. But it wasn't. It was a good, deep cut.

He looked around for Mike, his face all scrunched up, looking like Ron-Ron. I glanced down at the knife at his waist and thought about jumping him and sticking him with it. But I went on acting sorry and looking afraid, and that overwhelmed his stupid little mind and made him stand there, not sure what to feel or do. All I had to do now was stick to my lie that it was an accident.

As we headed back down to the cabin, I ran alongside him just to see if he would cry. Whenever he glanced over at me, I let him see the excitement on my face, as if seeing him crying was the best thrill in the world.

When we reached the fire truck road, Mike was coming up the hill, limping! Adam yelled out, asking what happened, and Mike said he had twisted it when we tripped him in the cabin. With each step, his big frame fell to one side.

The great and powerful Mike was limping. It was like the end of something.

He hobbled up to us, saw Adam's blood-streaked cheek, and looked at me. At that moment, I knew I was no good at being mean. Everything was backward. I hadn't meant to bring him his father. It was Adam. He wouldn't stop bothering me.

"It was an accident," I said.

He said nothing to me, but instead told Adam to wipe the blood off his face. While Adam bent down and started wiping with snow, Mike stood with his back to me. All I could do now was give him a chance to get back at me and hope he took it.

"Remember Mrs. Jessup?" I said. "My father cheated on Mom with her."

He looked at me, shook his head as if I was just a stupid little kid, and started limping down the road. Adam, his face wet from snow, was laughing at me again, back on the winning side. Following them, I thought of the worst things to say about my father.

"He used to hide brandy in his desk. That's how he got fired."

I ran up to Mike and said that I didn't believe a word of what was said on the radio. My mother didn't either. No one would. He gave me a flash of anger. Why did I keep talking about it?

I was all but crying. I said I wanted him to be sad for once. Why did he have to be so strong? I was tired of always getting the pity. What was wrong with wanting to give it for a change? Why couldn't he put down his father, too?

Adam's eyebrows were up as if I had just ruined myself a thousand times and not even he could enjoy this anymore. Mike just turned and limped on. I tried to egg on his anger.

"I know it's Piggy Peg Wilt."

He stopped.

"At least Mrs. Jessup wasn't a local," I said, trying to laugh about it.

He turned and limped back to me. I hoped he was going to punch me in the face, but in the calmest voice, all he said was, "What would your mom think, Josh?"

Adam laughed again.

"'Josh's brother fell off the cliff,'" I started yelling to make fun of myself, "and now he's nothing but a big, red stiff."

On the turn down to the cabin, Mike starting limping bad. I watched as he climbed up on his brother's back. I had never seen Mike needing anyone before. Adam, stumbling to one side, strained to hold him. As I followed in his deep, dragged out tracks, I couldn't take my eyes off the two of them hooked together, Mike's bad ankle dangling, Adam's legs wobbling to carry them both. It was more than piggy-back I was seeing. It was brothers.

Halfway down to the cabin, Mike fell off his brother's back, and in the tumble, he and Adam laughed the same hearty laugh they were known for, a laugh that said nothing fazed them, not a cut face or a twisted ankle, not something on the radio, that even in the worst moments there was something funny.

We found Ron-Ron down at the cabin, standing over under a tree, mumbling to himself. He wasn't violent like Adam, though he sure looked it, with his scrunched-up face and way of standing in one spot forever, twisting his hair up into a crown of thorny curls, saying weird half-dirty words over and over, like "dick suck" and "butt fart." He sure spooked the tourists in town doing this. Mike looked down at my old galoshes and asked if my feet were still cold.

When I acted huffy and didn't answer, he told Ron-Ron to carry me.

Ron-Ron came forward like Frankenstein obeying orders and bent down. But I didn't want to put my legs and arms around a retard. I wanted Mike. I had already said I was sorry. What else could I do?

The four of us headed through the snow, Mike riding piggyback on Adam, then Ron-Ron, then, about twenty yards behind, me. All the way down the mountain I had to listen to Ron-Ron drone, "Josh sad, Josh weak, Josh crying," while Adam went on laughing his heart out.

When I got home, Mom still had the radio on. It had been on all day, and she hadn't been able to turn it off. The same news about Mr. Wilkinson was on every hour, over and over. She was sick of hearing it, but at the same time kept hoping to hear more. School would probably be open tomorrow.

One look at me, and she knew something was wrong. I told her it was Peg Wilt, and she looked at me as if another shop full of precious old antiques had burned down.

"Peg Wilt?" she said. "Are you sure?"

I nodded with all the bitterness the day had given me.

"They told me."

She looked off into space, back into the same room then glanced back at me. "They told you? Oh, Josh, what have you boys been talking about today?"

I made it as bad as I could. I said Mr. Wilkinson fooled around on Mrs. Wilkinson all the time.

"He's always been that way."

Mom looked at me as if whatever I had heard today, I had heard too much.

"And they just talked about it with you?"

I nodded the biggest lie of my life.

Mom never talked to me about Mrs. Jessup. Instead, I had to listen to her and Dad fighting over her, especially to Mom's hysterical voice cutting through the floor like a corkscrew drill. When Dad moved out, Mom went to see Father Ron, but I had no one to talk about it. I wanted her to feel guilty about that now.

All evening I watched her looking at that space directly in front of her where she put everything she worried about.

"Well, I guess it's true," she finally said, "if they say so."

I told her that Adam had tried to start a fight with me over it.

"What about Mike?" she said. "He's still your friend, isn't he?"

I said nothing and that only upset her further.

"Well," she said late that night, "we'll certainly know what *not* to look for in our next superintendent."

# Lady In the Park

Her plain, older face keeps her safe, after dark, after midnight, while she skulks and lingers among the sweating shrubs, hanging black trees, and luminous grass in this dewy town park, in this dark, old village of Stonington. Why does she come here when the nighttime becomes a vacant, doorless world, where the inaccessible silhouettes of houses and steeples expose her to be the last person in this town still awake?

She seems the omega of human consciousness, an explorer at the back door of daylight, misplaced in the new millennium in her fiftyish office attire—a tailored, drab wool suit over a silk blouse. She creeps along the grassy knolls, under tall, ribbed spires and angular gables in this ancient New England town. She keeps a dog close to her, a bushy white terrier, its ratty mouth an unintelligible vault of grunts and whimpers. The little fella stands with a droop in his leash, and the downward strike of light upon it makes the leash look like a snow-rimmed power line. Both the lady and dog orbit here, under the oil lamps, under the misty umbrellas of light, having stepped lightly across the night in tranquil anonymity.

Her old-timey dress—her glazed and pinned hair, pancake makeup, and earthy, puritanical wool—hides her pain. She is forlorn, even though she is hearty in the cheeks and warmly layered. Even so, her heart is suffering.

She seems to work in an office resisting the onset of automation, for she looks worn by the years of having at her desk a wide array of handy office gadgets: a stapler, metal ballpoint pens, carbon paper, and a black rotary phone that rings like an expiring Westclock alarm.

When the town bell strikes midnight, she inches around the lampposts and benches and ivy barrels, stepping precisely on spots of light, her dog mimicking her. Then, under an ice-covered cinematic moon, a deranged smile breaks. Her dog turns, whimpering.

What evil does she hold as she roams the black axial world, letting her shadow replace her body? This black axial world of the surreal: telephone poles as robots, for example, guarding the houses, the twinkling backdrop of gaslit eyes watching her, and the corporeal shadows moving along the streets like windblown sheets of black tar paper.

Or perhaps an irrational red is what she sees, an angry shimmer upon all things, dead or alive. Maybe the chilling, syrupy darkness serves her an elixir, an absolute space free of the daytime, where she can see forever on the nightside of day.

Is she insane? Roaming the damp park so late at night? Or has she uncovered a life larger than hers? Do the roots of these dense black trees control the breath of trees and grass? What is she in the airglow of the sky?

No gentleman ever comes for her. Men leave her alone, and women rarely bring themselves to glimpse her from passing warm cars. So she stands here as a strange, unapproachable woman in her forties, looking behind her at a lifetime of ceremonies—when she moved north for college, when she married an untrustworthy man, and when she kept precise order to their needlessly large house.

In divorce, every precious thing of a home is lost—rich laughter, kitchen odors, the ambitious clang of pans, and the balance of furniture: love and dimension. The companion is lost, too. She shows his absence. At close range, a sudden leap of age shows. Under makeup, lines as fine and undiscoverable as cracks in old paintings converge at the outer corners of her eyes. Lint balls, of a lighter gray than that of her sweater, hang from her like debris.

"Oh, for land's sake," she mutters, thinking of the copper-handled skillet soaking in the sink at home.

Each night, whether the abstracted outdoors succeeds in tiring her mind into a passive unwind of thoughts, she ultimately prepares for the return home. She cannot cope with the large, silent house any longer. Years ago, she started sleeping on the sofa in the living room, in the glow of a kerosene space heater. Since then, her small body wrapped in a patchwork quilt has gotten ever smaller. She knows she is living less than life.

Oh, but the house is so worrisome, with its sticking cabinet drawers and rusted latches, its chipped, loose bathroom tiles and water stains in the ceiling where a pipe awaits the moment to burst. Blown bulbs in every room. All unjust annoyances. Not to forget the deserted wasp nests in the corners of the upstairs windows. Or the warped door, loose step, and cracked window. Now, she shivers from the damp air in the downstairs hallway, due to a recent gathering of ghosts.

Absolutely, she cannot go home.

The church towers down in town have darkened, and the bars have emptied. The town cop car passes once an hour. If she's spotted, she, with an agile turn of her black heel, quickly recedes into the dark drape of limbs, her dog nimbly following. Too sensible to sleep a night on a pigeon-poop-pelted bench, she is, for an hour or so after midnight, a woman without a residence, a cleanly dressed bum.

# Their Beloved Brimful Bubble Baths

When they opted not to manage the hotel during the summer season, neither had anticipated using a mispacked set of room keys to sneak into place two months later, into a room to take a long luxurious bath. In the New Year, when the hotel closed for three months, they, the winter caretakers, had soaked in a different bathtub each night. Inside the twenty-room Spanish pensione called the Libertad, they played a kinky game of hide-and-seek. He'd hid in one of the unheated rooms, and, soon enough, she'd find him in the dark, stripped, sudsy, silly, and soaking in the bathtub. She'd hurry and join him, and they'd cozy up in the warm, steaming water.

Once vacating their quarters at the hotel, they moved into a new colonial apartment across town. It reacquainted them to the placid privacy of a residence. Their apartment, one of the four in a refurbished clapboard colonial, offered endearing, innovative, concocted furnishings—doorways made from closets, a memorialized radiator framed and enclosed within a Formica kitchen cupboard, back-to-back decommissioned fireplaces, and a narrow Sears shower stall wedged inside a gutted closet, in a two-hundred-year-old side room overlooking the slate walks of the old New England town.

One complaint. One huge complaint. The bedroom in their apartment could not hold a king-size bed, and a queen-size filled the room wall to wall on two sides. They had not anticipated this shortcoming. So, after weeks of sleeping on a lumpy foldaway bed in their charming dollhouse apartment, they sorely needed a bathtub soak. Back rubs with pepperminty ointments and showers with limp water didn't cut it.

"I miss my bathtub!" she heard him complaining in their second month without floorfuls of buffed tubs around them.

She watched her husband towel himself as if grating cheese, peeved by the lazy showerhead softly dropping tame water.

"We can always go to my mother's," she suggested, having a mother who, on the sunniest Saturday of each month, telephoned to see if her only daughter would like "a mental health day" at the zoo.

"They have a big tub," she added.

Her suggestion was immediately yucky, weird, and upsetting. Sitting in water where his father-in-law—no, thank you.

"They won't be home Saturday or Sunday," she continued, and already the weekend, though distant, looked ludicrous, stealthy, and unsavory, spent secretly soaking in her parents' pedestalled bathtub.

Again, no, thank you.

Of course, they hadn't been serious about sneaking into the hotel. They and the owners had never related well, so any incident there, they knew, would transpire into an unlawful entry or a situation as disgraceful. Going to another hotel, say, one cheaper, was not a consideration. The Libertad or nothing. Paying the exorbitant high-season rate to their former employer for a room seemed inevitable.

In their three years at the hotel, bathing together had become a ritual for them, a way to cleanse more than their bodies, an emotional baptism of sorts, an ablution indulging in their favorite Crabtree & Evelyn bath gels—apricot and jojoba. Most of all, they had fun. In whichever room they choose—his favorite was 3-C, hers 4-G—they mounted the tub like bumper cars, he in the front seat, she in the back, her legs gripping his waist. At least once he licked her toes under the soapy water, and her legs recoiled like a prodded reptile.

"Ick!" she shrieked before retaliating by dishing handfuls of water in his face, much of which splashed out of the tub and soaked the floor.

Bombarded with water, he laughed all the more. He was still at the wheel. He regulated the spigot, and she sat helplessly pinned behind him.

As their shtick, they often quibbled over the warmth of the water: he liked it hot, she preferred just warm. Every evening, when she discovered which cold room he occupied, she quickly undressed and eagerly hopped into the water only to rebound onto the cold tiles, her legs and feet slinging water. Antsy and shivering, she refused to get in with him until he, sedated by the steamy heat, grudgingly added an inch or two of straight cold water, paddled it into the hot eddies behind him, and scooted forward, his heels hooking the spigots.

"Better?" he asked, fishing for the facecloth and apricot soap.

"Better."

They soaked quietly, droplets percolating from the points of their elbows, earlobes, and from the saturated and twisted ends of her hair, *plink, plink, plinking* into the water. If a streetlight illuminated them, they fancied their woven bodies as marble sculptures of lovers reposing in the fountain.

Then, with zesty precision, she'd add, "Oh"—high, fluffy cones of suds toppled from her palms as she dowsed her face—"I sold a three-hundred-dollar gold amethyst."

In the summer, the hotel was hopping with guests. In the winter, she worked part-time at a jewelry store while he stayed at the hotel during the day, upgrading rooms at the owner's direction—replacing pipes, applying fresh paint, and laying new carpet, all of which he could do quite well.

"Good, sweetie. I'm glad. I'm happy," he said, swishing the warm water around them, the moments restful, therapeutic, and intimate.

Every so often, he'd blast the hot water while draining an inch of the sinking tepid water. In this manner, they lay in a bathtub for nearly an hour each night, often in the absolute dark, their hands wrinkling, the suds flattening, the water cooling, and sometimes gushing abruptly into the overflow slit whenever they made waves.

"Let's get out now," he decided, swollen like a hot dog from the heat.

If she tried to stay, he tickled her toes and, as soon as one of them drew the curtain around the bathtub, the water games were underway—he heaving armfuls overhead, she skimming palmfuls into his ears, both of them kids at the end of the day, destressed and uncomplicated, silly and fun.

Four months passed in their new apartment. They were no longer silly and fun.

"Sure wish I had a bath," she admitted tonight, already early September, when they came home from a walk, more achy than weary, especially their ankles and heels.

They walked most evenings, zigzagging the historic town. Navigating the charming yet beveled brick walls quietly punished their feet, and, once reaching home, they often exclaimed that their strolls felt like hikes.

Tonight, once again, they settled for quick, lousy, lightweight showers.

"This does nothing at all," he griped, hopping out of the shower after a few seconds, dripping, leaving the water running, as if walking off a job. "I need to have a damn bath!"

What bothered them most about their shower was its pathetic size. Whenever they braved its smothering sides and packed themselves together into the glass stall, the low-hung corner showerhead and flaccid pressure prevented them from even sharing the water.

"Why doesn't this place have one bath?" he pressed, making them both more miserable.

He had soured over the matter, suspicious of a great personal injustice, of the world denying him an essential, the way he ranted if without his ailing car for more than a day.

Once, with his feet in pain, he improvised a bathtub of sorts by emptying her largest soap tin and filling it with the hottest water from the spigot to soak his feet.

"This isn't working either!" he fumed.

The cloudy tap water filling the tin proved not only too shallow to submerge the thumping balls of his ankles, but also leaked through the seams in the tin, soaking the hardwood floor.

"This is crazy!" he burst out, yanking his pink feet from the tin, water splattering on the TV Guide.

"Oh, honey, here, let me try some Ben-Gay."

She swirled fingertips of white, reeking cream into his ankles, enthusiastic about a quick cure. He, though, was a pill. Being smeared with a minty balm—greasy even though it claims to be greaseless—then waiting for its brief, smelly, chemical climax of a horrid feeling of chilly warmth, only aggravated him further.

"Shouldn't we just go, honey?" He straightened up in the chair, a deck chair taken from the hotel. "Let's just go."

Her eyes flashed, and she verified what sounded so magically romantic. "Back there—to the inn?"

While he drove, she checked their disguises—his burgundy attaché case, her black Coach bucket bag, both stuffed with whatever first came off the hangers. They had changed into vibrant polo shirts to look touristy.

"Wonder which room we'll get," she said.

Parked, they walked up the lit brownstone steps to the Libertad. They never met the summer help. At check-in, they were obviously nervous. When he produced a credit card, the robbing cost of a room and the adventure of treating themselves to a deep, luxurious bath competed for a moment, clashed a final time.

Up the stairs, they ran. He wanted the water as hot as they could stand it. She wanted to kiss under the suds. They both knew they would again cleanse more than their bodies.

# Every Living Thing

The windstorm, sneaking into town after dinner and blind-siding century-old oaks and elms, both upset and exhilarated Anne and Michael Thompson. Its torrid August bluster had miraculously spared the white poplars in the corners of their yard. But in the yards around them, the uprooted and defoliated maples and beeches displayed an impressive ring of wreckage, bringing TV vans and cameras into their neighborhood.

Except for shreds of bayberry shrubs blown to the edge of the grass and tinted with a silvery afterglow of life, their property had altogether missed damage from a waterless thunderstorm now balling itself into a hurricane just south of Cape Cod.

Anne and Michael bought their Chesapeake-blue, cross-gabled Craftsman house just last month, just in time for the July family reunion. Over a holiday weekend, the gathering started at her mother's place as usual, then broke into excursions to wherever sons and daughters made their lives close by. Michael and Anne's remarkable new house, with all its charming rooms and high windows, turned out to be an immediate family favorite. Unfazed by the storm, unshaken and untouched, the house debuted impressively, gaining a notch of family standing. It proved invincible, a true Thompson.

At the reunion last month, Uncle Gary, barely recognizable from his private grief over his divorce, commented that Anne's view of the sharply shadowed Victorians on her street reminded him of his ex-wife's hometown in upper Vermont. Anne, listening with half an ear, replied that their new house, located on a quiet street near an elementary school, only twenty minutes from Boston, guaranteed a high resale value. She worked in real estate. She knew.

In the aftermath of the storm, parents, siblings, and friends from all over phoned Anne, excited to chat with a survivor in the Parkwood Hills neighborhood, the hardest hit, mentioned on every channel.

"But we're fine," Anne gaily informed the callers.

Luckily, their porch swing, though tossed like a dinghy in the sea, had not gouged the new coat of blue on the clapboards.

After work the next day, she and Michael, chipper with the salubrious tang of another holiday weekend, walked through their neighborhood to survey the downed trees. Power company men in green hardhats were still limbing, sectioning, and hauling away tons of hardwood.

"Oh, look at that one, honey," Anne moaned, her voice rising with a hint of girlish thrill. "What a shame."

In a grove of evergreens along the unlined road ahead, a tall, slender pine stood broken at its center. The upper half had not plunged to the ground but instead stuck halfway down, in the branches of other trees. It appeared to rest in midair.

"That's awful," her husband consoled, his face tilted to the sky.

The open wood at the break flashed a fresh, searing wound colored like wheat glossed by wind. As they stepped closer, around dusty orange pylons and backhoes parked for the night, Michael pointed to where the severed tree, while falling, had sheared off a ladder of sizeable branches from the tree it now leaned against. The force of friction had raked away strips of bark. These fibrous, dangling sheaths, penetrated by the late afternoon sun, had pinkened like steamed skin.

"It'll probably die, too," he announced with grim fascination.

"You think so," his wife asked, aroused by his lustrous tone promising death. "What a shame."

On the street paralleling theirs lay a dusting of green leaves, some lying face up as almond-shaped spots of dark jade, others prone, their undersides tinted with a silvery-lemon hue, the phosphorous pulse of death. With the street plastered by a papery green mosaic, Anne wondered aloud if the town would sweep up the mess or if it would fall to the homeowners.

At the street's end, where the view of houses on the perpendicular avenue widened and brightened, an enormous elm had fallen dead like a dinosaur between two snobbish, stately Tudors. The sight filled Anne with shivers of deep satisfaction. She delighted in the misfortune of others, these prominent old-timers on this street, so rich and aloof. She envied them and their mansions. She now snickered at their misfortune. The elm, as huge as a culvert pipe, had thundered down on their plush, manicured lawn. Branches, flung violently, impaled the spotless, perfect lawns, scattering limbs and leaves yards away. Where the trunk had obliterated under strain, a fresh, jagged fissure of bright wood had exploded in a wide ring of shredded and flaky debris.

"Wow!" she and her husband sang out many times while freely moseying inside the disaster area, eyeing this monstrous reptile slain between the grand homes.

"That's terrible," she said. "How will they ever get all of it out?"

The tip of the elm, branched out like a Christmas tree, had bowed the wrought iron fence. As they moseyed around the area, they noticed that this gigantic slug of a tree had also flattened the head of the gazebo.

"They're lucky it didn't hit their house," she noted.

Their curiosity pulled them into town, past the hospital, the library, and the police station. Each intersection invited them into a maze of thrilling displays of destruction. Felled oaks wiped out stone walls laid a century ago. Savagely uplifted beeches, removed from the ground below the roots, left gaping holes in yards. Smaller limbs, amputated by the high winds, strewed the streets. From city hall to the high school, their town looked like the setting of an apocalyptic movie.

Cleanup, underway in places, exposed sides of buildings and views of yards as a close haircut reveals proportions of a face. The damage mortalized what had loomed for decades as organic statues flourishing through the seasons. The trees in their neighborhood, they realized, had been quietly living.

Walking faster than he, she eagerly absorbed the degrees of harm, guessing in thousand-dollar increments the compensation each conquered tree would earn. One tree had clipped a span of molded cornice on an apartment house, knocking away several dentils like a fist against teeth. That would bring a five-figure claim, she remarked.

When they reached the town park, an enormous, sawed-off tree trunk stood before them like a giant mushroom in an amusement park.

"That poor old tree!" she cried out, running toward the moist, gleaming disc the size of a grand rose window with tracery as precise as the tree rings. The surgical surface so captivated her that she stroked the pattern of concentric white rings, her index finger following the bands inward, her face ignited with wonder.

"Smell that?"

She breathed in the fragrance issuing from the wound. Then, with her hand cupped, she swept handfuls of sawdust onto the grass, where a bone-white paste of wood chips, spewed from a chainsaw, had turned doughy overnight in the dew.

At this point, her dim-eyed husband looked tired and reluctant to go farther. She admitted to him that the thrills were subsiding, both in ruin and in number. Plus, her feet, landing in shallow sailing sneakers, hurt.

"It's time to go home," she announced.

Three days later, after the last few piles of logs and limbs had been hauled from the streets, the Thompsons learned that Uncle Gary had died overnight from what doctors concluded to be a failed heart.

"He was on his way downhill for a long time," Anne's mother, Marge, remarked. Marge spoke with a zesty hint of private glory for her having flown to Columbus to help her older sisters with the funeral. They all stayed a few extra days to sort through Uncle Gary's house, boxing up whatever the three sisters agreed to take. Gary, they learned, had been drinking heavily in recent months, neglecting his poodle, Fritz, whom his wife had left him. He ignored his bills, as well as his flower garden, which he had always tended.

News of his death alarmed his niece, naturally.

"Oh, it's so terrible," Anne said.

But her mother was the celebrity this time. Gary was her brother. She, rather than her daughter, was receiving a flurry of calls from friends—from old Mr. Sullivan who had served with Gary in Korea, to an old school friend who spotted his name in the obituaries. In his local circle of acquaintances, each claimed Gary to be a fine man, his passing such a shame.

Anne offered to help in whatever way. In fact, she was eager. Hearing of Uncle Gary's demise infused her with a morbid interest in seeing how others closer to him were reacting, similar to her search of every street to see the destruction.

Talking to her mother about Uncle Gary, she fought to restrain the excitement seeping into her voice. His death had induced in her a grisly vigor to tally his life into an amount of compensation he had owed others but escaped the duty of repaying.

"What a shame," she found herself once again saying to her husband. "He really wasn't that old."

"It is too bad," he replied.

"I never really knew him," she admitted.

The next morning, at the edge of their yard, she spotted a leftover limb, its leaves no longer silvery as if glowing and living, but brown and wrinkled. Uncle Gary's existence had transpired like the fall of a tree, and like the massive tree trunk in the town park, his death left behind him the space he had occupied. This boundless area took only a day to forget.

# Acknowledgments

Grateful acknowledgment is made to the following literary journals in which these stories were originally published:

"Like Apes," *Berkeley Fiction Review*

"Genetic Drift," *Eureka Literary Magazine*

"Silver Balloons," *Identity Theory*

"Fourteen Seconds," *The North American Review*

"The Spirit in My Shoes," *ACM (Another Chicago Magazine)*

"Vineyards in a Far-Off Land," *Phantasmagoria*

"Marshmallow People," *Kenyon Review*

"Renting," *Terrain.org*

"Crows and Sparrows," *GW Review*

"Alone," *The Scruffy Dog Review*

"The Houseplant Generation," *Kansas Quarterly/Arkansas Review*

"Shadow Box," *Painted Bride Quarterly*

"The Last Sailor," *The MacGuffin*

"The Scratchboard Project," *Iowa Review*
    *Nominated for The Pushcart Prize
    *Received honorable mention in *The Best American Short Stories 2007*

"Memory of Distant Friends," *Sun Dog: The Southeast Review*

"Missing," *Alaska Quarterly Review*

"Electric Church," *Portland Monthly Magazine*

"Pictures," *Outerbridge*

"Short Lives," *Hudson Valley Echoes*

"We Never Liked Them Anyway," *Concho River Review*

"Lady in the Park," *RE: Arts and Letters*

"Their Beloved Brimful Bubble Baths," *Catalyst*

"Every Living Thing," *Westview*

---

My deep gratitude goes to Cornerstone Press publisher Ross Tangedal for discovering this collection and overseeing its superb publication. I especially thank the fine editorial team at the press who embraced this collection and sharply improved the stories: Brett Hill, Kirsten Faulkner, Kenzie Kierstyn, Anthony Thiel, and Grace Dahl. Thanks, also, to production directors Chloe Verhelst and Carolyn Czerwinski, media director Zoie Dinehart, and sales manager Natalie Rieter.

A very warm and special thanks goes to my sister Nancy C. Brooks as typist and proofreader; and to my colleagues Andrew Madigan, Samuel Waragu, and Rob Snyder for their professional guidance.

JOHN MICHAEL CUMMINGS is the award-winning author of three novels and over one hundred short stories. His debut novel, *The Night I Freed John Brown* (2008), won the Paterson Prize for Books for Young People. His short stories have appeared in *The Kenyon Review*, *The North American Review*, *The Iowa Review*, and *Alaska Quarterly Review*. He has been twice-nominated for the Pushcart Prize, and he received an Honorable Mention in *The Best American Short Stories* series in 2007. He holds a BA in studio arts and graphic design from George Mason University and an MFA in creative writing from the University of Central Florida. He lives in Harpers Ferry, West Virginia, where his family has lived for six generations.